Join the celebrations
with these sparkling Christmas novels from
MARY HIGGINS CLARK
and
CAROL HIGGINS CLARK

## SANTA CRUISE

"If you want a frothy, holiday-themed whodunit starring the affable PI Regan Reilly, her husband, and mystery-writing mother—all aboard a luxury liner's three-day maiden cruise—then this is your ticket."

—*Booklist*

"Full of mystery-lite cheer."

—*Publishers Weekly*

## THE CHRISTMAS THIEF

"A fun, speedy read."

—*Entertainment Weekly*

*Santa Cruise* is also available from
**Simon & Schuster Audio**

## HE SEES YOU
## WHEN YOU'RE SLEEPING

# DECK THE HALLS

"In their first collaboration, mother and daughter have produced a holiday confection."

—*The New York Times Book Review*

"Mary Higgins Clark and daughter Carol Higgins Clark create a winning detective duo by teaming up favorite characters from their own respective novels. . . . An entertaining . . . Christmas treat."

—*People*

"Fans will greatly enjoy the pairing of two favorite detectives—and two popular writers—in a Christmas ornament of a book."

—*Publishers Weekly*

"For fans of either of the Clarks, this book is a real treat."

—Bookreporter.com

"Some delightful Dickensian characters."

—*Providence Sunday Journal* (RI)

"The authors have created a wonderfully unique cast of characters."

—*The Pilot* (Southern Pines, NC)

BOOKS BY CAROL HIGGINS CLARK

# MARY
# HIGGINS CLARK

✴

# CAROL
# HIGGINS CLARK

# *Santa*
# *Cruise*

## A Holiday Mystery
## at Sea

Pocket Books

NEW YORK    LONDON    TORONTO    SYDNEY

Pocket Books
A Division of Simon & Schuster, Inc.
1230 Avenue of the Americas
New York, NY 10020

This book is a work of fiction. Names, characters, places, and incidents either are products of the author's imagination or are used fictitiously. Any resemblance to actual events or locales or persons, living or dead, is entirely coincidental.

First Pocket Books paperback edition November 2007

POCKET and colophon are registered trademarks of Simon & Schuster, Inc.

For information about special discounts for bulk purchases, please contact Simon & Schuster Special Sales at 1-800-456-6798 or business@simonandschuster.com

Cover image by Debra Lill

Manufactured in the United States of America

10  9  8  7  6  5  4  3  2  1

ISBN-13: 978-1-4165-3802-8
ISBN-10:    1-4165-3802-X

# Acknowledgments

The ship has come to shore. Our very special thanks to our fellow passengers aboard the Santa Cruise.

Our editors, Michael Korda and Roz Lippel.

Our agents, Sam Pinkus and Esther Newberg.

Our publicist, Lisl Cade.

Our copy editor, Gypsy da Silva.

Thanks to Sigal Miller of Mahwah, New Jersey, who suggested our title, *Santa Cruise.* Cheers, Sigal!

And of course our families and friends who saw us off and welcomed us home. A special loving tip of the hat to John Conheeney, the perfect shipmate always.

Finally, to all our readers . . . until next time. . . . Anchors Aweigh!

*In memory of Thomas E. Newton*

*A gentle man and our very dear friend*

*With love*

# Santa
# Cruise

# 1

*Monday, December 19th*

Randolph Weed, self-styled commodore, stood on the deck of his pride and joy, the *Royal Mermaid,* an old ship he had bought and paid a fortune to refurbish and on which he intended to spend the rest of his life playing host to both friends and paying guests. Docked in the Port of Miami, the ship was being readied for its maiden voyage, the "Santa Cruise," a four-day trip in the Caribbean with one stop at Fishbowl Island.

Dudley Loomis, his forty-year-old PR man, who would also serve as cruise director, joined Randolph on the deck. He took a deep breath of the refreshing breeze blowing off the Atlantic Ocean and sighed happily. "Commodore, I have e-mailed all the major news organizations once again to let them know about this unique and wonderful maiden voyage. I began the release, 'On December 26th, Santa is turning in his sleigh, giving Rudolph and the other reindeer some time off,

and taking a cruise. It's the Santa Cruise—
Commodore Randolph Weed's gift to a select
group of people who have in their own unique
way made the world a better place this past year.' "

"I've always liked giving gifts," the Commodore
said, a smile on his weathered but still handsome
sixty-three-year-old face. "But people didn't always
appreciate it. My three ex-wives never understood
what a deep and caring man I am. For goodness'
sake, I gave my last wife my Google stock before it
went public."

"That was a terrible mistake," Dudley said
solemnly, shaking his head. "A terrible mistake."

"I don't begrudge her the money. I've made
and lost fortunes. Now I want to give back to others. As you know, this Santa Cruise was created to
raise money for charity, and celebrate those who
have given of themselves."

"It was my idea," Dudley reminded him.

"True. But the money to pay for this cruise is
coming out of my pocket. I spent considerably
more than I expected in order to make the *Royal
Mermaid* the beautiful ship she has become. But
she's worth every penny." He paused. "At least I
hope she is."

Dudley Loomis held his tongue. Everyone had
warned the Commodore that he'd be better off
having a new ship built than dumping a fortune

into this old tub, but I *do* admit it cleaned up rather well, Dudley told himself. He had been cruise director on mammoth vessels where he had to worry about several thousand guests, many of whom he found intensely irritating. He would now deal with only four hundred passengers, most of whom would probably be happy to sit on deck and read instead of having entertainment shoved down their throats twenty-four hours a day. Dudley had come up with the idea of the Santa Cruise when reservations for passage on the *Royal Mermaid* were almost nil. He was a PR man right down to the rubber soles of his yachting shoes.

"We should have a free cruise the day after Christmas to get the kinks out of the ship before any paying passengers, or reviewers, come on board," he had told his boss. "You'll donate passage to charities and do-gooders. It'll only be a few days, and in the long run it will pay for itself with the good publicity I'll get for you. By the time our official maiden voyage rolls around on January 20th, we'll be turning people away. You wait and see."

The Commodore had needed a few minutes to think about it. "A totally *free* cruise?"

"Free!" Dudley had insisted. "Everything for free!"

The Commodore had winced. "The bar, too?"

"Everything! From soup to nuts!"

Eventually, the Commodore agreed. The special Santa Cruise would set sail in one week, the day after Christmas, and return to Miami four days later.

Now, as the two men walked along the freshly scrubbed deck, they went over the final details. "I'm still hoping for one of the television stations to at least attend the pre-sailing cocktail party on the deck," Dudley said. "I've sent word to the ten Santa Clauses you are treating to get here early so they can try on the lightweight Santa Claus outfits that you had made for them. They should be ready to mingle with everyone at our evening cocktail party.

"It turned out to be a blessing in disguise when I had that fender bender with that Santa Claus from Tallahassee last month. While we were exchanging insurance papers, he got weepy and confided how exhausting it was to listen to children all day long, have pictures taken with them, and, worse yet, be sneezed on. By the time Christmas Day rolled around, he'd be exhausted and unemployed again. That's when the light went on in my head to include ten Santas among the guests . . ."

"You're always thinking," the Commodore agreed. "I just hope we get enough paying passengers in the next few months to keep this ship afloat."

"It'll all be fine, Commodore," Dudley said in his most cheery cruise-director voice.

"You said we hadn't heard from all the people who won this trip at charity auctions. What's the status on that?"

"Everyone is coming—we're just waiting to hear from one passenger. She was by far the highest bidder at an auction for this cruise. I sent her a letter by FedEx, and as an enticement offered her the remaining two staterooms so she could bring friends. She's a good person for us to have on board. She won forty million dollars in a lottery, appears on television regularly, and is a contributing columnist to a large newspaper." He did not add that he had lost the name and address of this winner—who had attended his friend Cal Sweeney's auction—and had just followed up on it. He almost fainted when he realized Alvirah Meehan was not only a celebrity, but a columnist.

"Splendid, Dudley, splendid. I wouldn't mind winning the lottery myself! In fact, I may need to—"

"Good morning, Uncle Randolph."

They had not heard the Commodore's nephew, Eric, come up behind them.

Sneaky as always, Dudley thought as he turned

to greet the newcomer. I swear he could make his living as a mugger.

"Good morning, my boy," the Commodore said heartily, beaming at his kinsman.

The warm smile on thirty-two-year-old Eric Manchester's face was the expression he reserved for the Commodore and other important people, Dudley observed. With his perfect tan, sun-streaked hair, and muscled body, Eric had obviously divided his time between the beach and the gym. He was wearing a Tommy Bahama floral shirt, khaki shorts, and Docksiders. The sight of him made Dudley ill. He knew that when the passengers came on board Eric would be outfitted as an officer of the ship, although God knows what office he was supposed to hold.

How come I wasn't born good-looking, with a rich uncle? Dudley wondered wistfully.

"I'm running into town, sir," Eric addressed the Commodore, totally ignoring Dudley. "Anything you need?"

"I'll let you two chat," Dudley said, anxious to get away from the farce of watching Eric pretend he was of any use to the Commodore, the *Royal Mermaid,* or the upcoming Santa Cruise. Eric had wormed his way onto the payroll immediately after his uncle bought the ship.

The Commodore smiled at his sister's son.

"Don't need a thing I don't already have," he said heartily. "Have fun at the party you went to last night?"

Eric thought of the wad of cash he'd been given at that party, the down payment on what would make the Santa Cruise a risky and dangerous trip—and profitable for him . . . "It was lots of fun, Uncle Randolph," Eric said. "I was bragging to everyone about our upcoming Santa Cruise and how generous you are helping to raise money for charities. Everyone there wished they were coming with us."

The Commodore slapped him on the back. "Good work, Eric. Get people interested in us. Get people to sign up for one of our voyages."

I did, Eric thought, but you won't know about them . . . He shivered slightly, yet he couldn't help but smile at the irony.

Eric's guests would be the only two paying passengers on the Santa Cruise.

# 2

## Friday, December 23rd

At seven P.M. on December 23rd, a light snow was falling on New York City as last-minute shoppers and partygoers scurried through the streets of Manhattan. In the festively decorated Grill Room of the Four Seasons restaurant on Fifty-second Street, just off Park Avenue, lottery winners Alvirah and Willy Meehan and their good friends, suspense writer Nora Regan Reilly and her funeral-director husband, Luke, were all sipping glasses of wine. They were awaiting the arrival of Nora and Luke's only offspring, Regan, and her new husband, Jack, whose surname also happened to be Reilly.

The two couples had met exactly two years earlier, when Luke had been kidnapped by the disgruntled heir of one of his deceased clients. Alvirah had been a cleaning woman who had won forty million dollars in the lottery and then became an amateur sleuth. She had introduced herself to Regan and helped in the frantic search to save Luke. In the process, Regan had met Jack, who was head of the Major Case Squad in Manhattan, and they had fallen in love. As Luke wryly observed, "It's an ill wind that blows no one good."

Now, Alvirah, her ample figure smartly dressed in a dark blue cocktail suit, was bursting with the invitation she intended to extend to the four Reillys, but also trying to figure out how to make it an invitation they couldn't refuse.

Willy, her husband of forty-three years who, with his white hair, map-of-Ireland face, and generous girth, was the living image of the late, legendary Speaker of the House Tip O'Neill, had been no help to her on the cab ride over from their apartment on Central Park South.

"Honey," he'd said. "All you can do is invite them. They'll say 'yes' or they'll say 'no.' "

Now Alvirah looked across the table at petite Nora, elegant as always in a deceptively simple black dress, and six-foot-five Luke, towering beside her, his arm loosely around the back of her chair. We always have fun and excitement when we go on trips together, she thought, then realized that her idea of fun might be their idea of too much excitement.

"Oh, here they are!" Nora exclaimed as Regan

9

and Jack came up the stairs, spotted them, waved, and started over to the table.

Alvirah sighed with joy. She absolutely loved this young couple. Regan had her mother's blue eyes and fair skin, but she was four inches taller than Nora and had inherited her black hair from her father's side of the family. Jack, six feet two with sandy hair, hazel eyes, and a firm jaw, had an air of no-nonsense self-confidence that had made Alvirah sure from the get-go that he was the right man for Regan.

Jack apologized for keeping them waiting. "A few last-minute things came up at the office, but it could have been worse. I'm happy to report that as of now and for the next two weeks, Regan Reilly Reilly and I are at liberty."

It was the opening Alvirah needed. She waited until the captain poured wine for the newcomers, then raised her own glass in a toast. "To sharing a wonderful holiday season," she said. "I have a terrific surprise for the four of you, but first you'll have to promise you'll say 'yes.' "

Luke looked alarmed. "Alvirah, knowing you, I can't make a promise like that without hearing a lot more details."

"I wouldn't either," Willy agreed. "This is what it's about. We got roped into attending a charity auction. Need I explain more? You've been to plenty of them yourselves. Once they started the live auction after dinner, I knew we were in for trouble. Alvirah got that look on her face . . ."

"Willy, it was for a good cause," Alvirah protested.

"They're all good causes. Ever since we won the lottery, we've been on the list for every good cause known to man."

"It's true," Alvirah admitted with a laugh. "But I went to this one because it was being chaired by Mrs. Sweeney's son, Cal. She's the lady I used to clean for on Tuesdays. Cal is a trustee of their local hospital, and it needs help. Anyhow I got carried away, I admit, and I won a Caribbean cruise for two. I never heard another word about it and didn't realize it was a Christmas cruise. It's been such a crazy year that, to be honest, I forgot all about it until this afternoon, when a FedEx envelope arrived from a cruise director. There had been some kind of slipup, and the cruise I won at the auction is set for next week. It leaves on December 26th and comes back on the 30th."

"Three days from now! That's mighty short notice," Jack said. "Are you going to go? If not, you could probably force them to put you on a different cruise. It's their fault you didn't get sufficient notice."

"But this is a very special voyage," Alvirah explained eagerly. "They're calling it the Santa

Cruise. Everyone on board is someone who either won the trip by being the highest bidder in a charity auction; or who is a part of a group that did a great deal of good helping other people during the year; or who, after submitting proof of making a generous donation to a worthwhile charity, was selected in a random lottery."

"You mean no one's *paying?*" Luke asked incredulously as he accepted a menu from the waiter. "That cruise line must be rolling in cash!"

"I have the brochure with lots of pictures and all the details," Alvirah said, reaching down and fishing it out of her purse. "The ship looks gorgeous. It's brand new. Well, *almost* brand new—it was refurbished from stem to stern. If you can believe it, it even has a helicopter pad and a rock-climbing wall, just like all the new big ships. The best part is that the cruise director is so apologetic about the notification mix-up that he wants us to bring four people as our guests to make up for it, and he offered two luxury rooms with balconies— just like our cabin."

She beamed at the four Reillys. "I want you all to sail on the Santa Cruise with us."

"Oh, that's impossible," Nora answered quickly, shaking her head and looking at Luke to back her up.

"Aaaah, we're just planning to relax next

week . . ." Luke began clearing his throat as he tried to think of a stronger excuse.

"How better to relax than on a cruise?" Alvirah insisted. "Think about it. You two are going to the South of France after the first of the year. Regan, I know you and Jack are meeting friends to ski at Lake Tahoe on New Year's Eve. What do you have planned for those four days after Christmas that beats sailing in the Caribbean?"

It was a rhetorical question. "Regan," Alvirah continued, "I just heard from Jack's own lips that he's on vacation for two weeks. What are you committed to do the day after Christmas and the three days after that?"

"Absolutely nothing," Regan said promptly. "Jack, we've never been on a cruise together. I think it would be fun."

"The weather prediction for the New York area next week is freezing to frigid or the other way around, whichever is colder," Willy said encouragingly. He knew that in the couple of hours since that FedEx package arrived Alvirah had set her heart on having the Reillys join them on the cruise. "We're hiring a private plane to fly us to Miami on the 26th," he added, hoping that Alvirah wouldn't admit that this was the first she'd heard of *that* plan. "Think about it. A beautiful ship. Fine people as our fellow passengers. Swimming in the outdoor pool in December. Sitting on the deck reading a book. I'll bet lots of the people will be reading your books, Nora. What do you say?"

"It sounds too good to be true," Nora said matter-of-factly, but then she paused a moment and added, "I certainly know that we always have a great time with you guys, and I definitely would enjoy spending quality time with my child and brand-new son-in-law."

Alvirah smiled triumphantly. She could tell that the Reillys were going to go on the cruise with them. Nora and Regan were getting excited about it already and Luke and Jack would fall in line, however reluctantly. As they toasted to sharing the Santa Cruise, Alvirah was glad she'd never brought up the fact that yesterday, at yet another charity luncheon, she'd had a reading by a psychic who had been hired as a gimmick to raise extra money. As soon as her cards were dealt, the psychic's eyes had widened to the point that her eyelids had disappeared into her skull. *"I see a tub,"* she had whispered. *"A large tub. You are not safe in it. Listen to me. Your body must not be surrounded by water. Until after the New Year you must only take showers."*

# 3

## Sunday, December 25th

Under cover of darkness late on Christmas night, in the Port of Miami, a rowboat glided silently up to the side of the *Royal Mermaid*. A rope ladder was dropped from the lowest deck.

"You go first," Bull's-Eye Tony Pinto grunted as he grabbed the ladder and handed it over to his fellow escaping felon.

"You just want to make sure the rope is secure before you give it a whirl," Barron Highbridge said icily, as he stood unsteadily, put one foot up, tested the ladder, and began to climb.

"Hurry up!" a voice urged from above.

Larry the Creep, at the helm of the rowboat, extended a beefy hand to Bull's-Eye Tony. "Don't worry, Boss. We'll be waiting for you just offshore Fishbowl Island. We'll sneak you ashore, then you'll be home free. Now try to relax on this cruise."

"Relax? Hiding in a stateroom with that idiot

Highbridge for the next three days? I told you I didn't want to be on the run with anyone else."

"We were lucky to find this situation," Larry protested. "That poor dope Commodore Weed should only know what a louse he has for a nephew! Lucky for us, though. As soon as the cops find out your wife is wearing your ankle bracelet, they'll be swarming all over the country looking for you."

"I'll say that nephew is a louse—he has some nerve charging me a million bucks for a three-night stay."

"He wanted more," Larry reminded him. "I drove a hard bargain with him."

Bull's-Eye looked up. In the shadowy darkness he watched Highbridge effortlessly maneuver himself up to the deck and grasp the hand that was extended to him. His heart racing, Tony stood, grabbed the rope, and positioned his foot on the first rung. "Merry Christmas," he muttered bitterly and turned to Larry. "If you want to give me a present, find where the Feds hid that jerk who ratted me out and whack him."

Larry nodded.

"That would be a really nice gift," Bull's-Eye emphasized.

From above, sweating profusely, Eric watched Bull's-Eye begin to lumber up the ladder. Eric had been warned by Larry the Creep that if anything went wrong and Tony ended up in the clink, he would be swimming with the fishes.

Then Eric stared in horror as Bull's-Eye's gun slipped from his pocket and fell into the water. At least *that* wasn't my fault, he thought.

For two million bucks—one million for each stowaway—Eric had been willing to take this huge risk.

But now as a cursing, red-faced Bull's-Eye came closer and closer, grasped the rail, and heaved his thick body over the side of the deck, Eric realized that he might have bitten off more than he could chew. The other guy he knew he could handle. I should have stuck with white-collar criminals, he thought, trying to appear in charge as he whispered in what he hoped was an authoritative tone, "Follow me." He did not have to warn them to be silent. Most of the crew was already on board in preparation for the maiden voyage, but it was late and the ship was quiet.

Clad in hooded sweatshirts and dark glasses, the two felons followed Eric up a service companionway to the boat deck at the top of the ship. Eric peered out into the carpeted passageway. The coast was clear. He beckoned them forward. As they were passing the Commodore's door, something slipped from under Highbridge's sweatshirt and fell on the floor. Even though the carpet was plush, there was a distinctive thud.

"Oh goodness, my toiletries kit," Highbridge whispered, slipping as he bent down to grab the leather case. Quickly trying to steady himself, he accidentally bumped against the Commodore's door, barely missing the mermaid-shaped door-bell.

Eric's heart almost stopped. His uncle was a light sleeper and often spent much of the night reading. He raced down the passageway, the others on his heels, stopped in front of his stateroom, and with trembling hands inserted the key. The green light went on, the electronic lock beeped happily, and he pushed open the door. The two escapees followed him inside the room. Eric shut the door behind them and double-locked it.

The curtains to the balcony had been drawn for the night by the cabin steward. A mint was on Eric's pillow. Bull's-Eye Tony lumbered over and sat on the couch while Highbridge dropped his leather toiletries kit on the bed and sighed.

Some roommates, Eric thought. Tony, a dangerous crime boss, and Highbridge, born with a silver spoon in his mouth, who cheated other people out of their money just for the thrill of it. Both in their mid-forties. Tony, on the short side with a powerful build, balding, and a face that looked as if it had gone a few rounds in a prize fight, and tall, thin Highbridge with his dark brown hair, chiseled, aristocratic features, and a disdainful expression he had probably been born with.

A knock on the door sent shock waves through the room. Eric pointed to the closet. Tony and Highbridge ran to it and disappeared inside.

"Eric, are you there?" Commodore Weed called from the passageway.

Eric turned on the bathroom light and pulled his robe off the hook to suggest he'd been about to get undressed. The robe over his arm, he opened the door. Uncle Randolph was a sight to behold in his custom-made, blue-and-white pajamas, complete with a sailboat embroidered on the lapel. "Hi," Eric greeted his uncle, trying to sound sleepy.

"Mind if I come in?" the Commodore asked soulfully.

Eric had no choice but to open the door wider.

The Commodore stepped inside. "I heard a thump on my door and hurried into the passageway just as your door was closing. I guess you can't sleep either, huh?"

In his long history of shady dealings, Eric had learned early on that it was always better to stick as close as possible to the truth. "I went for a walk on the deck, so keyed up about our Santa Cruise.

Then I realized how tired I was. I think that's why I accidentally bumped against your door." He yawned, then watched in horror as the Commodore picked up Highbridge's toiletries kit off the bed, and sat on the couch where the indentation from Tony's generous behind was still fresh.

"Handsome kit. I don't think I've ever seen you with it before."

"I've had it a while," Eric answered lamely and deliberately yawned again.

"I won't stay long," Randolph said in a tone that suggested he was just getting wound up. It reminded Eric of his long-winded high school graduation speaker who spent the first fifteen minutes at the podium mumbling, "Now before I start my remarks, I'd like to mention . . ."

"It's okay, sir, stay as long as you like," Eric said weakly.

"Insomnia," Randolph began. "The good thing about it is it gives you time to read. The bad thing is it gives you too much time to think. Tonight I was thinking about Christmases past when you were a little boy." He laughed. "You were a terror. Your mother almost died when she realized that you'd stolen the change out of all her guests' coat pockets at her annual Christmas party." The Commodore laughed again. "But that was a long time ago." He looked around. "I'm glad these luxury rooms turned out so well. It's nice to have a couch and a couple of chairs, not to mention a balcony. The closet is big, too, isn't it? A woman's dream." He got to his feet. "Tomorrow's a big day. We'd both better try and get some rest."

"Uncle Randolph, I want to thank you for making me a part of this wonderful new venture of yours."

"Blood is thicker than water, my boy," the Commodore intoned as he patted Eric on the shoulder, then crossed the room. The closet door was at a right angle to the outside door of the cabin. By mistake he put his hand on the closet door and began to turn its handle.

Eric lunged forward and threw his arms around his uncle's back. The Commodore let go of the handle, turned around, and wrapped his nephew in a bear hug. "I never thought you were an emotional fellow," Randolph said, his voice husky. "As a matter of fact, I thought you were something of a cold fish."

"I love you, Uncle Randolph." By now Eric was so nervous that his voice was quivering. His uncle obviously thought that he was about to break down and have a good cry.

"I love you too, Eric," the Commodore said softly. "More than you'll ever know. This will be a good trip for us. For our relationship. Now get some rest."

Eric nodded and quickly opened the cabin door and eased his uncle out. He stepped into the passageway and watched until his uncle's paja-maed figure disappeared into his own suite. Stepping back inside, Eric almost collapsed with relief. He double-locked the door and opened the closet.

"I need a hanky," Bull's-Eye whispered, then mimicked, " 'I love you, Uncle Randolph.' "

"I did what I had to," Eric said impatiently. "There's a queen-sized bed and a pullout couch. How do you want to arrange this?"

"I'm taking the bed," Bull's-Eye ordered. "You two can share the couch."

Barron looked at him, about to protest, but the sight of Bull's-Eye's ugly expression immediately changed his mind.

Eric spent the night twisting and turning on the lounge chair on the balcony.

# 4

*Monday, December 26th*

On a freezing cold December 26th, Alvirah,
Willy, Regan, Jack, Nora, and Luke met at Teter-
boro Airport to board the private plane Willy had
hired to take them to Miami for their Santa
Cruise. On the way down, they chatted about how
they had spent Christmas Day. The four Reillys
had gone to Jack's parents' home in Bedford,
where his six siblings and their families had all
gathered for the holiday.

"Here we are two only children with an only
child," Nora marveled. "It was so much fun to celebrate Christmas with a big group. Jack's family
are such nice people. Every single one of them."

Jack raised an eyebrow and smiled. "I assure
you, they were all on their best behavior. What did
you guys do, Alvirah?"

"We had a wonderful day," she said heartily.
"We went to midnight Mass on Christmas Eve,
slept late, then had dinner at a really good

restaurant on the Upper West Side with Sister Cordelia. She's the only one of Willy's sisters who lives in the area. We took her, five or six other nuns, as well as some of the people Sister Cordelia knows who don't have much family. There were thirty-eight of us and it was really grand."

*"Thirty-eight?"* Jack exclaimed. "That's more than my mother had."

"Well, they'd be out of luck if I had to cook for them," Alvirah said. "We had a room to ourselves and ended up singing Christmas carols."

"It's a good thing we had a room to ourselves," Willy interjected. "Next year, Sister Cordelia wants to bring a karaoke machine."

Alvirah leaned toward Regan. "That's a beautiful necklace," she said admiringly. "I bet it's a Christmas present from Jack."

"Alvirah, anytime you'd like a job in my office, it's waiting for you," Jack said with a smile. "That necklace is actually a miniature Reilly crest."

"Complete with diamonds on a gold chain," Alvirah said. "I love it."

"Nothing too good for Reilly Reilly," Jack said.

When they arrived in Miami, the sun was shining brightly and the air was hot.

"Alleluia," Luke said as they stepped off the

plane. "This feels wonderful. These last few days I felt as if I would turn into an icicle."

The limo Alvirah had ordered was waiting for them when they exited the terminal.

"We have plenty of time to get to the ship," Alvirah said. "How about a nice lunch at Joe's Stone Crab? If we get to the ship by three, it'll be just the right time to check in."

"Alvirah, boarding starts at one," Willy objected.

"And it goes until four. Let all the anal types get settled in, then there will be no line by the time we get there."

Everything is going exactly according to plan, Alvirah thought with satisfaction, as the limo pulled up to the terminal where the *Royal Mermaid* was filling up with the Do-Gooders of the Year. They got out of the car and, as the driver unloaded their luggage, stared out at the ship. An enormous Christmas wreath with the words SANTA CRUISE in the center was hanging from the bow.

"I kind of expected this ship to be a little larger," Willy said. "But I guess I was thinking about those huge ocean liners that carry thousands of people."

"It looks perfectly lovely," Nora said hastily.

"The brochure said the *Royal Mermaid* accommodates four hundred passengers," Alvirah noted. She waved her hand dismissively. "That's plenty."

A porter with a cart came up to greet them. "Go right in the terminal," he said. "I'll take care of your bags."

All three men reached for their wallets. "I've got it," Luke said firmly.

They stepped inside the terminal where two security stations were set up.

"I just hope they don't want me to take the pins out of my hair," Nora murmured. "They did that to me at Kennedy Airport when we were going to London. I looked like Gravel Gerty when I got on the plane."

But the whole group passed through with flying colors. They walked down a hallway to the departure area where a line of clerks was waiting to check in the guests. It quickly became clear that most of the other passengers had already boarded. There was no one on line at any of the counters. Three men in blue blazers, white slacks, and gold braided caps had just emerged from the gangplank to the ship. The eldest one spotted them and rushed over.

"Welcome! Welcome! Which one of you is Alvirah Meehan?" he asked. "We were so afraid you'd changed your mind about joining us. That would have been such a disappointment."

"A big disappointment, indeed," one of the other men echoed.

"I'm Alvirah and this is my husband Willy and our friends . . ." Quickly she introduced them.

"And I am Randolph Weed, your host. But my friends call me Commodore, and I love it. And this is my nephew, Eric Manchester, and my cruise director, Dudley Loomis. Let's get you checked in and on board. The opening cocktail party will be over in twenty minutes. We sail at four."

"At four?" Alvirah said. "My information said six. I have it right here—"

Dudley sprang into action. He wasn't anxious to see his signature on the letter she was about to pull out. He'd been frazzled when he wrote that letter to her. "Let's get you checked in," he urged, leading them over to the counter where all six clerks were waiting. Luke and Nora began to check in with one, and Jack and Regan with another. The Commodore and his nephew were hovering protectively around Alvirah and Willy.

"We're going to have such fun," the Commodore was saying. "A most fascinating group of fine people together on the high seas for four days. I promise you you'll love every minute . . ."

The clerk took Alvirah's and Willy's names and typed them into the computer. She frowned and started tapping away at the keys. "Oh my," she said.

There can't be a problem, Dudley thought. There just can't.

"I don't understand how this could have happened . . ." the clerk said.

"What?" Dudley asked, trying to keep a smile on his face as the Commodore's expression became stern.

"The room assigned to the Meehans is already taken. And every other room on the ship is filled." She looked up at the Commodore, Dudley, and Eric. "What are we going to do?"

"There are no other rooms?" the Commodore asked, glaring at Dudley. "How could this have happened?"

I must have miscounted, Dudley thought. I should have just offered to let them bring one other couple.

"Alvirah," Regan said, "Jack and I will spend a couple of days in Miami and then fly out to Lake Tahoe. We don't mind at all."

"Absolutely not!" the Commodore barked. "No such thing. We have available one of the most luxurious rooms on the ship that the Meehans will find most comfortable. It's right next to my quarters." He looked at Eric. "My nephew will happily spend this cruise in the guest bedroom in my suite. Isn't that right, Eric?"

Eric felt the blood draining from his face.

There was only one thing he could say. He said it. "Of course."

"I'll have your things moved in a jiffy," Dudley said brightly. Even though he was nervous about his mistake, it was an exquisite pleasure to inconvenience Eric.

"Eric, I hate to put you out," Alvirah said. "Take your time packing your stuff. We'll go up to that cocktail party right now and enjoy a drink until we set sail. Then we'll be happy to settle in."

Eric managed a smile. "I'd better get packed up so they can freshen the room," he said. "I'll see you all later." He turned on his heel and like a shot was up the gangplank.

"What a nice young fellow your nephew is," Alvirah said to the Commodore.

# 5

The Welcome Aboard Santa Cruise cocktail party had been in full swing for more than an hour. Most of the four hundred guests had had a second glass of champagne, some had had a third glass, and a few even more. You can tell who *they* are, Ted Cannon thought as he put down his own untouched flute. The band had been steadily playing holiday music. They swung into "Santa Claus Is Comin' to Town" for at least the fourth time. Here I am all alone, he reflected sadly. Ted had gone around to hospitals and nursing homes playing Santa Claus in Cleveland for fifteen years, something he'd been talked into doing by his late wife, Joan. She had been gone for more than two years now, but as a tribute to her he'd kept up the practice. Then someone had entered his name in the Santa Claus drawing for the cruise, and he'd been one of the winners. He still found it hard to believe.

Ted always closed his accounting office in Cleveland the week after Christmas, and in the old days he and Joan used to go on a vacation after spending Christmas with their son, Bill, and his family. Ted had been with them for the last few days. When he'd won the cruise, they had urged him to take it.

"Dad, Mom would want you to go out and have some fun. With nine other Santa Clauses on board, you'll have something in common to talk about. And if there are any single ladies on board, ask someone to dance. You're only fifty-eight, and you haven't even glanced at a woman since Mom died."

But now, standing in the midst of all these strangers, Ted felt desolate. He wondered if it was too late to grab his bags and get off the ship. He gave himself a mental shrug. *And what would I do then?*

*Snap out if it,* he told himself, and picked up his glass of champagne.

Ivy Pickering had just read the guest list and was thrilled to learn that Alvirah Meehan, Regan Reilly, and Nora Regan Reilly were all going to be on the ship. She had a glass of champagne in her hand and had positioned herself so that she'd see them the moment they arrived at the party. She wanted to introduce herself so that later on, when everybody got settled, she might be able to spend some time with them. She had been a fan of Alvirah's ever since Alvirah had started writing a column in the New York *Globe* after winning the money in the lottery. Ivy was so fascinated by Alvirah's account of how she and Regan and Regan's new husband, Jack, had worked together to save Regan's father when he was kidnapped.

Ivy was a new member of the year-old Oklahoma Readers and Writers group, whose members volunteered their time teaching people to read. Many of the writers were in the mystery field. Ivy was one of the readers. She always said she'd make a good detective but not a good writer. There were fifty in their group and they'd been written up in a magazine because of the amount of time they gave to literacy programs. That's why they had been invited to join the cruise.

For fun, the group had decided to have a ghost of honor, Left Hook Louie, an Oklahoman mystery writer who—after he retired from the ring as a heavyweight prizefighter—had begun punching out words. He'd written forty mysteries featuring a retired boxer turned sleuth. Louie had died in his sixties, and his eightieth birthday would have been two days from now, which was why they had decided to honor him. They planned to hang posters of his battered, smiling face, his hands in boxing gloves, resting on the typewriter, throughout the ship.

Ivy had never been on a cruise before and intended to explore every inch of the *Royal Mermaid*. Her eighty-five-year-old mother didn't get around much anymore but loved to hear all the details of Ivy's adventures. They lived together in the house where sixty-one years ago Ivy had been born.

As the Commodore led their group to the deck where the party was being held, Alvirah was looking forward to getting her first glimpse of the rock-climbing wall that had so intrigued her in the brochure. She was momentarily startled when a small, birdlike woman darted out at her and put a hand on her arm.

"I'm Ivy Pickering," the woman volunteered eagerly. "I'm such a fan. I've read your columns and every single one of Nora's books. I cut out pictures of Regan's beautiful wedding and saved them. I just knew I had to say hello to all of you the moment you got here." She beamed at them. "I won't keep you."

You *are* keeping us, Commodore Weed thought, but he wouldn't dream of offending one of his benevolent guests.

"I want to get a good place along the railing to watch as the ship begins to sail. But I wonder if sometime in the next day or two I could pose for a few pictures with you to show my mother when I get home?"

"Absolutely," Nora answered for all of them. Ivy Pickering nodded happily and rushed away.

A man with a camera on his shoulder was being led in their direction by an energetic young woman with a microphone. Her first question was for Nora. "What do you think of the idea of Commodore Weed honoring people who do good?"

Regan could swear she heard her father murmur, "She's against it." She knew that if there was one thing her father couldn't stand it was a stupid question.

Nora was saved from answering by the arrival on deck of two police officers. They were heading straight for the waiter who was approaching their group with a tray of champagne and a dorky smile. When the waiter saw the whole group staring, he turned his head to see what was of such interest. When he caught sight of the policemen, he dropped the tray, spun around, and ran down the nearest companionway to the lower deck. Before his pursuers even reached the companionway, they all heard a loud splash.

"Man overboard!" Ivy Pickering yelped.

The Commodore looked down at the mess at his feet. *Why did I waste my money on the good stuff?* he wondered mournfully.

Everyone ran to the rail to observe the activity below.

"Boy can he swim fast!" someone remarked.

Seconds later the wail of an approaching police boat suggested that no matter how fast the former waiter swam, he would be plucked from the water before he could make his escape.

Other waiters were rapidly scooping up the broken glass and mopping the deck. The Commodore hurried across to where Dudley, enveloped in a safety harness, had been about to give a demonstration of the rock-climbing wall. "I don't know what the problem could be," Dudley stammered. "He wanted the job *so* much and said that he used to work at the Waldorf."

"For all we know he's an ax murderer," the Commodore snapped. "Who else did you hire on faith?" The microphone where he had made his welcoming address was in front of the rock-climbing wall. He picked it up.

"Well, well, I promised you an exciting cruise . . ." But it took a few minutes to get everyone's attention. They were all fixated, watching the progress of the escapee. The Commodore repeated himself and added, "And we certainly seem to be embarking on an exciting cruise, heh, heh, heh." He paused. "Yes indeed," he finished lamely.

A young officer approached the Commodore and whispered something in his ear. The Commodore's worried frown began to ease. "I see. Perfectly understandable. Some women have no patience." He turned to the crowd. "The poor fellow was a bit behind on his alimony payments, it seems. No threat to anyone. He took a chance on love, and, oh well, 'tis better to have loved and lost . . ."

The Commodore had to restore the feeling of conviviality. "Now let's refill our glasses and turn our attention to the rock-climbing wall behind me. Our cruise director, Dudley, will demonstrate for us the fun you can have as you imagine you're climbing Mount Everest."

With a flourish, he turned to Dudley. "Reach for the stars," he ordered. Dudley bowed as deeply as he could, considering the fact that he was in the harness. The crew member assigned to hold the safety rope picked it up with a noticeable lack of enthusiasm.

Dudley put his right foot on the lowest prong attached to the wall and began his climb. He reached above his head, grabbed another prong, and started to pull himself up.

"Don't *you* try that," Willy whispered to Alvirah.

"Right foot, left foot," Dudley muttered to himself as he started to break a sweat. His right foot was searching for the next prong when he felt the one supporting his left foot start to wiggle like a loose tooth. "This can't be," he moaned.

But it was.

As he tried to hoist his weight onto his right side, the left prong gave way and fell to the floor. Both of Dudley's feet lost contact with the wall, and he began to sway back and forth on the rope like a would-be Tarzan.

The crowd yelled their encouragement. He attempted to smile, looked over his shoulder, then landed with a thud on the deck as the crewman let him down too quickly.

Nora and Regan did not dare look at their husbands.

# 6

After he learned that he had to vacate his room, Eric's feet barely touched the gangplank as he rushed back onto the ship.

He could have strangled Alvirah Meehan!

"Take your time packing."

Sure, lady. He *had* no time! He knew that that jerk Dudley was thrilled that he was being displaced. All this was Dudley's fault. He had messed up the room count. Now Dudley, cruise director extraordinaire, would be sending an army of stewards to complete the eviction process. I *know* he hates me, Eric thought, especially since I got a bigger room. Dudley had a small room without a balcony, but if only I had that room now, I could make do. Eric realized that he was scared to death to face Bull's-Eye and give him the bad news.

Not wanting to wait for the elevator, he bounded toward the companionway.

How am I going to hide them? *Where* am I

going to hide them? How can I possibly keep them in my room in Uncle Randolph's suite for *three days*? That guest bedroom is so small. And so is the closet.

All I know is that I have to get them out of my room, and fast.

"Ho! Ho! Ho! Eric!" one of the passengers called to him. "When do I get my Santa Claus suit?"

"Ask Dudley!" Eric snapped, as he hurried past. Then a thought occurred to him. He should get his hands on two of those suits. Bull's-Eye and the Bean Counter, Barron Highbridge, could put the Santa suits on, and nobody would become suspicious if they ran into them in the passage-way.

Where *were* the suits? They had to be in the sup-ply room on Deck 3, he decided. All of the Santas' staterooms were on Deck 3. The people who gave of themselves got lesser accommodations than the people who donated money. The way of the world.

Do I have time to go there? Before he could make a rational decision, Eric found himself heading for Deck 3. His set of master keys in-cluded a key to the supply room. Please let the suits be there, he prayed.

Eric could hear voices in some of the staterooms as he passed them. He must not be seen near the supply room. Passing the luggage that was still piled outside various stateroom doors, he pulled the keys out of his pocket and turned a corner. Way down the corridor he could see two people, but fortunately their backs were to him. He took giant steps to the supply room, put the key in the lock, turned it, and pushed open the door.

To his delight, the Santa suits were hanging on a clothes rack. He quickly picked two of them that looked as if they might fit a short, portly Bull's-Eye and a tall, thin Barron, two people who only gave gifts to themselves. He grabbed two white beards, two stocking caps, and two pairs of black sandals. The tropical Santas, he thought. In a cabinet he found a stack of black plastic garbage bags. He jammed all of the Santa paraphernalia into one of them. Time was running out. He was already sweating profusely.

He left the supply room and raced up the companionway to the Boat Deck. He made it to his room without having to explain to anyone why he was carrying a trash bag. The DO NOT DISTURB sign was still there. He opened the door and braced himself for the stowaways' reactions.

Barron was stretched out on the pullout couch watching television and eating from a bag of potato chips. "Shhhh," he warned Eric and whispered, "Tony just fell asleep. He's been very cranky all day."

"Well, he's going to get a lot crankier," Eric snapped. "I've got to move you two."

Tony's eyes flew open. "What?"

"There was a screwup. They're one cabin short. A couple of passengers are moving into this cabin."

"How cozy!" Bull's-Eye snapped. "Do you have any bright ideas about where you're going to put us?"

Barron sat up, a look of terror on his face. The bag of chips flipped over, scattering on the sofa bed and on the floor. "You told us this was going to be so easy. That we'd just stay in your room."

"You *are* going to stay in my room. The new one is down the passageway."

"Down the passageway?"

"In my uncle's suite."

"As in 'I love you, Uncle Randolph'?" Tony growled.

"The very one." Eric dumped the contents of the garbage bag on the bed. "Put these on," he said, his tone desperate. "Then we'll go into the suite. My uncle's not there. If someone sees us they won't be suspicious because there are ten Santa Clauses on this cruise."

41

There was a knock on the door. "May I assist you with your packing, Mr. Manchester?"

Eric recognized the voice of Winston, the pompous butler whom Uncle Randolph thought would give this operation some class. "No thank you," Eric called out. "I'll be another fifteen minutes or so, then you can prepare the room."

"Very well. Just ring for me when you're ready. Cheerio."

"Does he think he's in Buckingham Palace?" Tony hissed.

The imminence of possible discovery propelled both felons to move fast. They quickly undressed and pulled on the costumes. Eric handed them the beards and the caps. The sandals were loose fitting with adjustable straps. They looked ridiculous.

Tony's heavy-lidded eyes looked malevolent over the mass of white covering half his face. On Barron's face the beard hung loosely, covering most of his mouth. But at least if someone spotted them, there was a chance of their getting away without arousing suspicion.

"I'll see if the coast is clear," Eric said, his heart pounding. He opened the stateroom door and looked both ways. All was quiet. "I'll go down and check the suite and make sure no one's there." He walked down the passageway, opened his uncle's door, and took a quick survey of the rooms inside the suite. He then hurried back to his own room, opened the door, and nodded to the two men.

They followed him down the passageway and into the Commodore's suite. Breathing a sigh of relief, Eric shut the door. "The guest room's over here," he said.

"You've got to be kidding me," Tony growled when he got a look at the room. The only furnishings were a double bed, a night table, and a single chair in front of the built-in desk and storage cabinets.

Barron opened the door of the closet. "You expect us to hide in here?" he asked.

"No," Eric snapped. "Get in the bathroom."

Like the closet, the guest bathroom was much smaller than the one in his stateroom.

"Wait in there until I get all my stuff moved in," Eric continued. "Lock the door."

With a look of murderous fury, Tony nodded. "I'm warning you, Eric. We'd better not get caught."

# 7

Promptly at four P.M., the *Royal Mermaid* began her Santa Cruise out of the Port of Miami. By then, a thoroughly frazzled Commodore felt a little relief after grilling Dudley about how so many things could go wrong before they had even shoved off. Not getting a satisfactory answer from an equally frazzled Dudley, he headed for the bridge. He stood beside Captain Horatio Smith as the captain fired up the engines. It was reassuring to be in Smith's presence. After a mandatory retirement from a small but excellent cruise line, the seventy-five-year-old Smith had happily accepted the offer to be at the helm of the *Royal Mermaid*.

"All aboard, Commodore?" Smith asked.

"Minus one," the Commodore said grimly, not knowing he was actually plus one. "I just hope I won't have to pitch in and wait tables myself." Standing with Smith, who hadn't done anything stupid yet, the Commodore felt his good humor begin to return. Every maiden voyage has its ups and downs, he realized. The Commodore had been disappointed by the anguished expression on Eric's face when he was told he had to give up his room and move in with his uncle. He seemed so anxious to share this time together when we visited last night, the Commodore thought. One would think that he'd be happy to be even closer to me. We'd have more time to share. Oh well.

The Commodore turned to see how many people might be standing at the Peek-a-Boo window, which allowed passengers to watch the captain as he steered the ship. Another disappointment. There was only one observer, Harry Crater, a sickly looking fellow. In fact, he looks like he's about to keel over, the Commodore thought. When I chatted with him at the cocktail party, it was a relief to hear that he owned a helicopter, and if he had a medical emergency, he would send for it immediately. I wouldn't wish him hard luck, but perhaps a passing medical problem requiring the helicopter would be a newsworthy item. It would highlight our ability to respond to emergencies by having our own landing pad. He made a mental note to point that out to Dudley.

The Commodore waved and saluted.

At the Peek-a-Boo window, Harry Crater waved

back. It was the feeble movement of a powerful arm that was being concealed by a jacket two sizes too large. He didn't care about anything except the heliport, and that was obviously satisfactory for his plan.

Remembering to lean on the cane, he shuffled away.

The Commodore watched him depart. *His health may be failing, but clearly his spirit has not been broken. I just hope this cruise is of benefit to him. I wonder how much good he did for the rest of the human race this year. I must ask Dudley,* he told himself.

"Would you like to push the button?" the captain asked, a twinkle in his eye.

"Indeed!" the Commodore replied. Like a baby with a toy steering wheel, he slapped his hand down on the toot button.

*Tooooooooot! Tooooooooot!!*

"We're on our way!" the Commodore cried joyfully. "And there's no turning back!"

# 8

Regan and Jack's stateroom was at the opposite
end of the passageway from Luke and Nora's. It
was a deck below where Alvirah and Willy would
be staying.

The six of them had checked out both of the
Reilly rooms, found them satisfactory, and went
up to Eric's former quarters together. They were
all dying of curiosity. The room was in a separate
section of the ship, down the passageway from the
Commodore's suite, not an area where passengers
would normally stay.

The door to the room was open.

"Hello," Alvirah called as she reached the doorway.

A straight-backed, balding man in a dark
steward's uniform was running a cloth over a night
table. "*Good* afternoon, Madame," he replied with a
slight bow. "Are you Mrs. Meehan?"

"Yes, I am."

"My name is Winston. I will be your butler on this voyage. It will be my pleasure to ensure your absolute comfort. I am prepared to serve you everything from breakfast in your suite to a hot chocolate at bedtime. May I add my apologies for your inconvenience because of a reservation mishap?"

"No problem," Alvirah said heartily as she walked inside and looked around admiringly. "You guys have nice rooms," she told the Reillys, "but this one really takes the cake."

"It's terrific," Regan agreed. She had not missed the expression on Eric Manchester's face when he was told he had to give up the room. I can see why he wouldn't be happy, she thought. But it was more than that. He seemed *agitated*.

The closet door was open. Nora glanced into it. "The closet is practically a room unto itself," she commented.

"With all Alvirah's luggage, she needs whatever space she can get," Willy said. "Oh, here are the bags now."

An out-of-breath porter had arrived at the door.

"We'll clear out and give you a chance to get settled," Luke said. "Remember, there's a lifeboat drill at five o'clock."

Winston gave a quick last-minute inspection of the room, then shook his head. "How did I miss these?" he said under his breath as he leaned over and picked up several squashed potato chips from the floor by the couch. "I thought Eric was such a health nut . . ." As he straightened up, he said, "I think everything is shipshape for you now. Anything else you need, just pick up the phone please." He looked at the Reillys and sniffed. "Shall we leave the Meehans to unpack in peace?" His voice was at its most plummy and British, like a maritime Jeeves.

"We shall," Jack said dryly. *He calls himself a butler*, he thought. *Give me a break. We don't need to be told it's time to go.*

"Here's your hat, what's your hurry?" Luke mumbled.

"We'll meet you downstairs after the lifeboat drill," Alvirah said quickly, attempting to smooth over Winston's arrogance. "Isn't it wonderful that we're on our way?"

As the others followed Winston out the door, the porter struggled to hoist Alvirah's suitcases on top of the bed. Willy's garment bag was a marvel of efficiency. Except for one other smaller bag, everything he needed was in it. Alvirah opened the drawer of the night table next to her side of the bed and placed calcium pills in it. She had heard they were better absorbed if you took them at night. A deck of playing cards was inside the drawer.

"Ohhhh. Look at these, Willy. Remember how we used to like playing cards? We've gotten away from it these last few years."

"That's because you're too busy solving crimes," Willy commented.

The cards were held together with a rubber band. Alvirah picked them up.

Willy glanced at them. "I'll ask that guy Eric if they're his. Bad enough we took his room."

He stuffed them in his pocket. "If they make us sit too long at that lifeboat drill, we can always play Hearts."

# 9

While Regan was putting away the last of her clothes, Jack hooked up their computer. They had agreed that neither one of them wanted to be out of touch with the outside world for long. Even though they'd only left New York this morning, they already felt that their normal life was a million miles away.

The headlines of the day flashed on the screen.

"Famous Felons Flee!"

Jack whistled as he read the story:

Mob boss "Bull's-Eye" Tony Pinto and white-collar criminal Barron Highbridge are among the missing. The two men, from different worlds, were both due in court this morning. They were allowed to spend Christmas with their families, but obviously did not stay for leftovers. At Pinto's palatial home in Miami, authorities found his wife asleep in bed, wearing his ankle bracelet. "I don't know how it got there," she explained. "I'm a heavy sleeper. Where's my Tony?"

At Highbridge's estate in Greenwich, Connecticut, the Christmas tree lights were still burning, but no one was home. His eighty-six-year-old mother, whom he had claimed was terminally ill, was vacationing on the French Riviera with a group of her girlfriends. "We're having such a good time. We call ourselves 'The Golden Girls,' " she chirped over the phone. "It was a dreadful mistake that the jurors found my son guilty. He's got a good heart. He's made a lot of money for people over the years. . . . I feel *fine*. Why do you ask?"

Highbridge's longtime girlfriend is in Aspen with B–list actor Wilkie Winters. "I won't have anything to do with a convicted felon," she said piously, flashing the jewelry Highbridge is known to have bought for her.

Regan was reading over Jack's shoulder. Her fingers played with the necklace he had given her for Christmas. "I hope I'm never going to have to say that about *you*," she joked.

Jack gave her a look and they both continued to read.

Based on his wealthy family's impeccable reputation, forty-four-year-old Highbridge was able to attract numerous gullible investors in his Ponzi scheme. He was convicted of stealing millions of dollars from them. He was about to be sentenced and was expected to receive a minimum of fifteen years in prison. The trial of Bull's-Eye Tony Pinto, charged with ordering the murder of rivals in the construction business, was to have begun on January 3rd.

Jack shook his head. "Those guys both knew their goose was cooked. I had dealings with Tony when he was up in New York, but we could never get enough evidence to present to a grand jury. I was glad to see one of his guys ratted him out."

Regan sat on the bed. "They've got to be headed someplace where there's no extradition. But they'd have to have surrendered their passports as a condition of bail."

"With security so tight they won't get away with phony passports," Jack said. "I'll see what the office knows about it." He picked up his international cell phone and dialed. Keith, his number one guy, picked up on the first ring.

"Jack, you're supposed to be on vacation," he said when he heard his boss's voice.

"I am on vacation. I'm also looking at the Internet. I see Bull's-Eye Tony has flown the coop. I'll never understand why they didn't keep him in jail. If anyone's a flight risk, he's it. Have you heard anything about him or Barron Highbridge?"

"An informant claims that Pinto was trying to make contact with someone who could get him out of the country. The Feds have the airports covered. It's possible that either or both of them might be heading to one of those places in the Caribbean that has no extradition treaty with the United States."

"Is Fishbowl Island one of them? That's our only stop."

"I've got a list," Keith said. "Let me take a look." He laughed. "Guess what? Fishbowl Island *is* on it. So keep an eye out for Tony."

"We will. Anything else going on?"

"No, Boss. Relax and have a good time with your bride. How's the cruise ship anyway?"

"Don't ask," Jack said with a laugh. "One of the waiters jumped ship while we were still in port. He was arrested for nonpayment of alimony. And the cruise director fell off the rock-climbing wall."

"Sounds like you'll be safer on your skis this weekend."

"Maybe so. Keep me posted about anything I'd want to hear."

"Which is everything," Keith cracked. "I'm sure we'll be hearing lots more about Pinto."

Jack stared at the photograph of Pinto, which had just come up on the screen. "I'd hate to see him get away. He's as bad as they come."

As he closed his cell phone, an announcement came over the loudspeaker. "Attention Santa Cruisers! Commodore Weed here. We are about to have a mandatory lifeboat drill. All passengers must attend. No excuses. The life this drill saves may be your own. Grab your life jackets, and please don't trip on the belts. Crew members are ready to direct you to the dining room, where you will receive general instructions, then be led to your lifeboat station. Let's not have any Nervous Nellies—this drill is just a precaution."

Regan opened the closet door, pulled out the two life jackets, and handed one to her husband. "Do you think this is the only time we'll be putting these on?" she asked jokingly.

"With the way things are going, I wouldn't count on it," Jack said as he helped pull Regan's life jacket over her head. "You even look good in fluorescent orange."

"You liar. Let's go."

# 10

At least the lifeboat drill had gone well, Dudley thought, as he stood in the supply room, waiting to hand out the Santa Claus suits. Except for that idiot who thought it was funny to keep blowing the whistle on his life jacket.

I wish that the safety instructions didn't have that new advice that if you can't reach a lifeboat, you should put one hand over your mouth, hold down the shoulder of your life jacket with the other hand, and pretend that you're just walking off the ship as you jump into the water. It was ridiculous. Walk or jump you're still hitting the water in a most unpleasant way. That kind of talk scares people—I know it scares me. I can just see myself standing on the rail with the ship going down, and trying to delude myself I'm out for a stroll.

Dudley shrugged his shoulders. There was enough to worry about without borrowing trouble. If anything else goes wrong I may be walking the plank anyhow, he thought. I cannot believe the Commodore was so mad at me this afternoon. Was it my fault that that waiter didn't pay his alimony? No. Was it my fault that that first prong on the rock-climbing wall fell off? No. The Commodore should have been thrilled that I escaped with only a few bruises on my buttocks. I could use a good soak in a tub, he thought, but of course *my* room doesn't have a tub. I'm lucky it has a sink.

But I *did* hire the waiter, he admitted to himself. And the screwup on the room was an honest mistake. When I received the letter from Mr. Crater's nurse showing me the receipts for all the money he had given to charity this year, and saying that his final wish was to be with good people like him on this cruise, how could I refuse? I just wish I had written it down when I gave his name to the reservations people. Maybe I didn't get the final count straight, but it's their fault for assigning two people to the same room!

"Okay to come in?"

The first Santa Claus had arrived. "I'm Ted Cannon," he said.

He's one of the quiet type Santas, Dudley thought. He doesn't seem like a barrel of laughs. I can't picture him saying, "Ho! Ho! Ho!"

"Great to see you, Ted," he said in his most enthusiastic voice.

The Santa Clauses had been told that as a condition of coming on the cruise, they'd be expected to wear a Santa outfit at the first and final dinners at sea. Dudley was turning over in his mind how best to present the Commodore's newest idea—that he'd love to see them wearing the outfits as often as possible. The Commodore wanted his passengers to enjoy a festive atmosphere, having no idea that Santas all over the ship at all times would more likely drive his guests out of their minds.

The other nine Santas arrived within the next two minutes and crowded into the supply room. In those two minutes, Dudley had perfected his speech. Don't let them think they're doing us a favor, he reminded himself—let them think they're being honored by being chosen to work.

He felt relief as the men began to smile when he told them how proud the Commodore was to have them all aboard. "He wants to put the spotlight on the good you have all done to create warmth and joy for so many people during the holiday season," Dudley explained, thinking that some of the Santas probably promised kids presents they didn't get. "Because the Commodore understands how much love you provided to children of all ages when you wore your Santa outfits, he was hoping that you'd want to spread that love as often as possible during the cruise by wearing these outfits." Dudley pointed to the rack. "As often as possible," he repeated. His voice rose. "Morning, noon, and night."

The smiles vanished. Bobby Grimes, the roly-poly guy from Montana, who looked as though he should have been the cheeriest of all, said, "I thought this was supposed to be a free trip, thanking us for all the work we already did. Some thanks. When I work as Santa Claus, I get paid Santa Claus wages. This is a rip-off. What you call a breach of contract."

The troublemaker of the group has just identified himself, Dudley thought. I wouldn't put it past him to make a ship-to-shore call to one of those lawyers who advertise on TV. "Did you fall? Or almost fall? Maybe you suffered psychological damage when someone gave you a dirty look. We'll sue for you. You deserve it."

Some of the others were nodding and agreeing with Grimes.

"I've been wearing a Santa costume since Halloween," one of them griped. "I'm sick of it. I wanted to sit in a deck chair in a pair of shorts, not spend all day in a hot, scratchy suit."

"No good deed goes unpunished," another

Santa chimed in. "I was a volunteer Santa. I didn't get a nickel for traipsing around lugging a heavy sack over my shoulders."

Ted Cannon felt sorry for Dudley, but the last thing he wanted to do was wear the costume every night at dinner. In the two holiday seasons since Joan died, the Santa appearances were painful reminders that she was gone. She had always accompanied him to the nursing homes and hospitals, and afterward they'd go out for dinner together. Joan had laughingly insisted on paying for dinner those nights, he remembered. She'd said that Santa deserved a good meal after squeezing down so many chimneys.

"I agree with Bobby," Nick Tracy from Georgia drawled. "I'll wear the suit tonight and the last night, and that's it."

Ted saw the look of desperation on Dudley's face and decided to help out. "Come on," he urged the others. "We're enjoying a free trip. What's the big deal about putting the suits on for an hour or two a day?" He pointed to them. "They're even lightweight."

Dudley wanted to kiss him.

"But look at those beards," Rudy Miller from Albany, New York, pointed out. "We're supposed to eat with them on? Are we on a liquid diet?"

"You can take them off while you eat," Dudley

promised. "What we really want to do is let people take pictures with you."

Ted Cannon walked over to the clothes rack and began to check the sizes of the outfits. "These look as if they're cut pretty big," he commented. "I guess I'm a long." He removed one hanger, folded the contents over his arm, then took a beard, stocking cap, and sandals from the boxes next to the rack.

"I like wearing a Santa suit," Pete Nelson from Philadelphia piped up. "I was always a bit shy, but wearing the suit made it easier to talk to people. My therapist said it was like being an actor. He said that many actors are really very shy when they're not playing a part."

"He sounds brilliant," Grimes snapped. "Who cares whether actors are shy? Most of them are overpaid jerks."

"I resent that," Nelson said. "I'm just trying to share what my therapist is teaching me."

"Well, most therapists are overpaid jerks as well," Grimes countered.

Nelson frowned. "I really don't think you're cut out to be a Santa."

"You're right. This was my last season."

Maybe next year he should play Scrooge, Dudley thought. We're off to a great start. Why did I ever think up this Santa Cruise? This will turn me into a confirmed landlubber. He began to hand out the suits. By the time four of the Santas had taken them, there were only four left on the rack.

"I can't understand it," Dudley said, his voice alarmed. "We're missing two suits. Mr. Grimes, unless I can track them down, you will be relieved of your obligation to spread good cheer on this cruise."

"What?" It was clear that Grimes was caught off guard. The truth was that he loved dressing up as Santa Claus.

Ted Cannon sized up Grimes as the type who always complained no matter what. "Maybe we can rotate some of the suits. I'm in the cabin next to Pete. We're about the same size. We can share one."

"My therapist would be proud of you," Pete Nelson said with a smile.

"Mr. Grimes, if you wish you may share a suit with Rudy. Or you won't have to wear one at all, if you don't want to," Dudley sniffed.

"Whatever. I'll work it out with Rudy," Grimes said begrudgingly.

When the Santas left, eight of them carrying outfits, Dudley scoured the supply room. Not only had the two suits vanished into thin air, but the sandals, beards, and stocking caps to go with them were also definitely gone. Why would anyone else want them, and how am I going to explain having only eight Santa Clauses to the Commodore?

Who could have gotten into this supply room? It was always kept locked, so it had to have been someone with a key.

Dudley got nervous. I didn't have that waiter checked out, he thought. As a matter of fact, I didn't check *anybody's* references. We all know that most references are given by people who are forced to do a favor for their unemployed friends and most résumés are a pack of lies.

Someone on the ship was up to no good. Dudley didn't know whether it was a passenger or a crew member.

What Dudley *did* know was that if something else happened, it would be his fault.

All of a sudden, walking off the ship didn't seem like such a bad idea.

# 11

"Oh, I sail the ocean blue, and my saucy ship's a beauty," the Commodore sang, as he looked in the mirror over the couch of his sitting room and smiled at his reflection. His new uniform, a resplendent midnight blue tuxedo with gold-braided epaulets on the shoulders to match the buttons on the jacket, struck exactly the note he was hoping to achieve. He wanted his guests to view him as both a commanding presence and a genial host.

But it would be nice to have another opinion, he decided.

"Eric!" he called.

The door to the guest room was closed and locked, a gesture the Commodore felt was a trifle unfriendly. After all, he reasoned, with this large living room between the bedrooms, it's not as if we're crowding each other. Closing the door was one thing, locking it another. Certainly Eric couldn't think I would barge in on him? When I tapped on the door a few minutes ago and got no response, I only wanted to peek in to see if Eric had been catching a cat nap. I simply wanted to warn him that it was getting late. But the door was locked, then Eric called out in a very cross voice that he was stepping out of the shower and what did I want?

Maybe he *should* have taken a nap, the Commodore thought. He looked terribly tired today, and he certainly was cranky. Well, I know that he shares my concern that the voyage goes well from now on despite a few bumpy patches at the outset. . . .

There was a knock on the outside door of the suite. The Commodore knew it would be Winston with his plate of fancy hors d'oeuvres. I much prefer enjoying them here in my suite with a glass of champagne than munching on them while I'm shaking hands and posing for pictures with the guests, he thought. Nothing worse than a crumb on the chin or a dab of mustard on one's cheek when posing for a photo. People should feel free to point out offensive particles of food stuck to another person's face, no matter how exalted the position of the stuckee.

"Enter, Winston," he called out.

Winston entered the room in dramatic fashion,

a tray with an open champagne bottle, two glasses, and two plates of hors d'oeuvres held over his head. A small smile played on his lips, indicating that he was very pleased with himself. But then he always was. He placed the tray on the coffee table and ceremoniously poured a glass of champagne for the Commodore.

The Commodore inspected the selection of hors d'oeuvres—tiny potatoes sprinkled with caviar, smoked salmon, baked mushroom puffs in pastry shells, and sushi with dipping sauce. His face darkened.

Winston looked alarmed. "Are you displeased, sir?"

"No pigs in a blanket?"

A horrified expression came over Winston's face. "Oh, sir," he protested.

The Commodore slapped him on the back and laughed heartily as he settled on the couch. "Only jesting, Winston. I know you would drop dead before you would ever serve such a middle-brow item. But they *are* tasty."

Winston didn't comment, but he obviously didn't agree. The same selection of hors d'oeuvres had been placed in all the guests rooms, a gesture that Winston felt was surely unappreciated by most of the cruisers. They'd probably have preferred popcorn, he thought. He placed one plate of hors d'oeuvres on the table and picked up the tray. Then he turned and began to cross the room. Before he had gone six steps the door of Eric's room opened. Pulling it closed behind him, Eric gave the Commodore a blinding smile as he hurried to sit beside him on the couch.

"Sir, I hope I didn't sound unpleasant a few minutes ago when you called me." He tried to laugh. "Fact is, I stubbed my toe in the shower. I'd just been muttering something I won't repeat when I heard your voice."

"That's perfectly all right, my boy," the Commodore assured him as he bit into a mushroom puff. "It did enter my head that you sounded a bit cross, but a stubbed toe is the very devil." A slight frown creased his forehead. "You're not dressed for the evening. You're running rather late, aren't you?"

Winston placed the second plate of hors d'oeuvres and a glass of champagne in front of Eric. I wonder if he'd rather have more of his potato chips, Winston thought disdainfully. I'll have to inspect his room when I turn the bed down. The last thing I want is him ruining the Commodore's guest bedroom with hidden junk food. It's also interesting, Winston thought, that for someone who claimed to have just stepped out of the shower. Eric had put his daytime uniform back on. "Mr.

Manchester," he said, "Is there a problem with your dress uniform? Does it need pressing? I'd be happy to take care of it for you."

"No," Eric snapped. "I haven't showered yet."

"But I thought you stubbed your toe when you were showering," the Commodore said.

"I was getting ready to shower when I stubbed it," Eric corrected himself quickly. "I knew you were waiting to have a glass of champagne. I didn't want to keep you waiting."

"Very well." The Commodore turned to Winston. "That will be all, my good man."

Winston's bow was pointedly aimed at the Commodore. "You have but to beckon, sir."

The Commodore beamed at Winston's departing figure. He drained his glass of champagne and stood up. "I must run," he declared. "Try not to be too long, Eric. I count on you to charm our guests." He winked. "Especially the ladies."

Eric did not miss the note of admonition in his uncle's voice. He knew he was being told that he ought to have been ready to join the passengers now. He also didn't miss the way Winston had eyed him with nosy curiosity. "I won't be but ten minutes, sir," he said. He stood up and made a gesture of starting toward his room. Then as soon as the Commodore left the suite, he dumped the two hors d'oeuvres his uncle had not eaten onto his plate.

Bull's-Eye had been complaining about being hungry. Maybe this will hold him over, Eric thought, with increasing desperation. It was safe enough to leave those two in my room during the boat drill. But now I've absolutely got to get them out of here until Winston has turned down the bed and changed the towels. What a dope I was to say I had stubbed my toe in the shower. Winston can tell I'm nervous. He'll be sure to poke around in my room. And I can't leave Bull's-Eye and the Bean Counter in my bathroom. If Winston found that door locked he'd send for the engineer pronto.

These were the thoughts torturing Eric as he raced into his room to meet the cold stare of his two stowaways. Both of them, still wearing the Santa Claus outfits but without the beards and stocking caps, were sitting side by side on the bed.

Eric handed the plate to Bull's-Eye. "As far as food goes, this is the best I can do for now. I've got to get you out of here right away." The tone of his voice was somewhere between a direct order and a plea for understanding.

Both men just stared at him.

"I have a place for you that's sure to be safe."

Eric's words were tripping over each other. "The Chapel of Repose is on this deck. Nobody will go there. Then, after dinner I can sneak you back in before my uncle comes upstairs."

"You call this dinner for us?" Bull's-Eye demanded as he reached for a piece of sushi.

"No. No, I'll get you more. I promise. Please, we've *got* to go. Winston has a TV in his pantry. If I know Winston, he's in there polishing off the rest of the champagne and watching *Jeopardy!* That's what he does in my uncle's house. He's a nut for *Jeopardy!* Took the test to get on the show and almost made it. *Come on!*"

"Your price for getting us out of the country just went down," Highbridge snarled. "You're not getting another dollar from either one of us."

"And if anything happens and we don't get to Fishbowl Island safely, the orders to my people are to have you whacked." Bull's-Eye's tone was calm. He might have been saying, "Pass the salt."

Eric opened his mouth to object, but the protest died on his lips. Why did I ever listen to Bingo Mullens? he asked himself as his mouth went dry and his hands went clammy. He told me he knew an easy way to make big money. What had Bingo said? "Your uncle has a boat. He trusts you. I figured out a no-brainer."

Bingo had been arrested for illegal gambling in

Miami last year and had met Bull's-Eye in the lockup before both men posted bail. A month ago he'd contacted Bull's-Eye and told him he had a safe and sure way of getting him out of the country before his trial started. Bull's-Eye went along with it, to the tune of one million dollars. Bingo's cousin was a gofer for Highbridge in Connecticut. That's how Eric had made that connection. Now they're both sitting in my room, and unless I can keep them hidden we'll all be arrested, and that will be the *least* that will happen to me, Eric thought, his heart racing.

He had to keep the two men hidden for the next thirty-three hours.

Knowing that his very life depended on that gave Eric courage. "Put on those caps and beards," he ordered briskly. "Let's go!"

Eric checked to see if the coast was clear. The corridor was empty. He waved to the two of them to follow him. His final instructions were whispered with a nervous tremor that made his voice come out as a squeak. "Remember, if people see you, they *expect* to see Santas roaming around the ship. Don't try to run away from them."

Highbridge cursed under his breath.

He's changed, Eric thought. There was something in his voice that was both chilling and threatening. Eric's instinct was immediately justified when Highbridge said, "My people will get you if Tony's don't do the job. Count on it."

It took less than a minute but felt like hours before they were in the corridor that terminated at the Chapel of Repose. Eric pulled open the heavy wooden door, flicked on the light, and glanced inside. The chapel was the Commodore's pride and joy. It had an arched ceiling with stained-glass windows on either side. A carpeted center aisle separated six rows of white oak pews and led to a raised area suggesting a sanctuary. The altar, a long table covered by a floor-length velvet cloth was the focal point. An organ was off to the side.

"Get in," Eric said quickly, then shut the door behind them. "Go sit on the floor behind the table. If you hear the door open, scoot under it. I'll be back as fast as I can after dinner."

"Make sure you bring food when you get back," Bull's-Eye ordered as he ripped off his beard.

"I will. I will." Trying not to break into a run, Eric turned off the light, left the chapel, and hurried down the corridor.

Alvirah and Willy were waiting for the elevator. "Oh, glad to see you, Eric," Willy said. "Alvirah found a deck of cards in the night table by the bed. We were wondering if they were yours?"

"No, they're not," Eric snapped. Trying to soften his tone, he moved his lips in an attempted smile and said, "Even as a kid, I was always an outdoor guy. I could never sit still long enough to play cards."

"Well, then I guess I'll see if I can get a card game going on the ship," Willy said.

Five minutes later when he was in the shower, a thought hit Eric like a thunderclap. Bull's-Eye had slept in the bed. By any chance did the deck of cards belong to him?

And if so, would he want them back?

# 12

The predinner cocktails were being served in the spacious Grand Lounge adjacent to the dining salon. At the entrance, a photographer had set up his camera and a backdrop showing the railing of a ship against a star-spattered sky. There, at eight P.M., the Commodore would begin to pose for pictures as the cruisers filed into dinner.

The walls of the lounge were decorated with a variety of framed articles and photographs, all of which were a testament to the philanthropic efforts of the honored guests. One woman, Eldona Dietz, had been chosen because the newsy Christmas letter she sent out detailing every single activity of her children's lives for the past twelve months had won an award from a family magazine. An enlarged and framed version of the letter was displayed prominently on the wall. To make sure no one missed it, a smaller version was a centerpiece at all the cocktail tables.

The Commodore was speaking in a low voice to a flustered-looking Dudley, and it was obvious he was not happy with whatever Dudley was saying.

"The reason we only have eight Santa Clauses here is because two of the suits are missing, sir." Dudley had planned to try to find the perfect moment to break that news, but unfortunately the Commodore had already counted the bearded and costumed figures Ho-Ho-Hoing through the room and instructed Dudley to tell the other two to hurry up and get in there.

"How could two suits be missing?" the Commodore demanded. "The door to the supply room was locked, wasn't it?"

"Yes, sir."

"Was the lock picked?"

"No, sir."

"Then unless I'm delusional, someone with a key entered the supply room and stole the costumes."

"That would seem to be the case, sir." Dudley watched as the Commodore made a visible effort to control the outrage that was making his eyes send out sparks.

"My feelings are hurt, Dudley. Someone is trying to ruin our Santa Cruise. My blood is beginning to boil. This should have been reported to Eric if you couldn't find me."

"Sir, by the time I knew the suits were missing you were dressing for dinner, and I haven't seen Eric since the lifeboat drill ended."

"He was in my suite. I don't know what's keeping him now. He should be here. Not a word of this to anyone! I don't want the guests to get wind of the fact that we have a thief in our midst. They've already witnessed one of our waiters trying to escape arrest. Where did you hire these people from? A penal colony?"

"Yes, sir, I won't discuss this and no, sir, I didn't hire our employees from a penal colony. . . ."

Across the room, the four Reillys were sitting at a cocktail table. Regan was observing the byplay between the Commodore and Dudley. "I think Commodore Weed is giving the cruise director a hard time," she commented.

"He's the guy who fell off the rock-climbing wall, isn't he?" Luke asked.

"Yes, and I gather he was in charge of hiring that waiter who jumped ship."

"How did you find that out already?" Jack asked.

"When we were sitting around waiting for the boat drill instructions to start, you and Dad were debating who would be the nominees in the next presidential election. I overheard a couple of the junior officers talking about the guy who took the dive off the ship—"

"And I thought you were hanging on my every word," Jack said.

Regan ignored the interruption. "Those junior officers said the hiring was a joke. Dudley never did the hiring on the other cruise lines where he worked. It's not the job of the cruise director. They said he had to do it because the Commodore's nephew, Eric, the guy whose room Alvirah ended up in, was supposed to handle it and didn't. Dudley got stuck with finishing the job at the last minute on top of having to handle the guest list."

Jack pulled the newsy Christmas letter from the centerpiece. "The guest who wrote this must be really interesting. 'In the last twelve months it's been so exciting to watch Fredericka and Gwendolyn blossom into lovely young ladies. Violin lessons, gymnastics, singing, dancing, bird watching, etiquette classes, baking organic fatfree pies, etc., etc. . . . But all their activities have not prevented them from being conscious of their fellow man. We have a number of elderly neighbors whose doorbells they ring every morning to make sure they survived the night. . . .'

"Thank God they don't live in our neighborhood," Luke drawled. "These kids aren't on the ship, are they?"

"Don't look now," Regan muttered as two young girls ran past their table, a matronly woman in pursuit, calling out, "Fredericka! Gwendolyn! Give Mommy and Daddy back their champagne glasses!"

Jack tucked the newsletter back into the centerpiece. "Regan, promise me we'll never send out one of these."

"Duly noted," Regan agreed.

Nora had been studying the poster-sized picture of Left Hook Louie that was hanging on the wall nearest their table. "He was the nicest guy."

"Who?" Luke asked.

"Left Hook Louie," she explained, as she pointed to the poster. "He was a prizefighter who became a best-selling mystery writer. I did a signing with him when I was new and he was well established. He had a long line and I only had a few stragglers. He stood up and said to the crowd that he had read my book and loved it and anyone who didn't buy it should step aside and go a round with him right then." Nora laughed. "I sold a hundred books!"

Regan and Jack stared up at the poster. They both had the same thought. Left Hook Louie bore a startling resemblance to Tony Pinto, whose picture they had just observed on the computer screen.

"Do you know if he had any kids?" Jack asked Nora.

"Not to my knowledge," Nora answered. She glanced at the door. "Oh good, here are Alvirah and Willy."

The Meehans, Willy in a tuxedo like all the other men and Alvirah in a white silk jacket and long black skirt, were coming across the room and heading toward them.

"Sorry!" Alvirah said. "But for once I'm not the one who's late. Willy started playing solitaire and was convinced he could beat himself. By the time he knew it was a lose-lose situation, he only had a few minutes to get ready. Isn't that right, Willy?"

"You're right as usual, honey," Willy said amiably. "Alvirah found a deck of cards in the night table drawer, and I started fooling around with them. They're not new, so we figured they belonged to the Commodore's nephew. But we just bumped into him at the elevator, and he told us he hates cards. I've got them in my pocket in case anyone wants to play later."

The Commodore started tapping against the microphone and blew into it. "Attention! Attention! It's time to give out the Santa Cruise medals to all of you who have given of yourselves so generously this past year."

"First I'd like to call up everyone from the Readers and Writers group. It humbles me to be in their presence. . . ."

Dozens of hands shot into the air, waving empty glasses to signal the waiters for a refill. It was clear that the Commodore was just warming up. One by one, he placed medals hanging from ribbons around the necks of each member of the Readers and Writers group. All the people who had donated to charities, including Alvirah, were next. Finally, when the medal was placed around Eldona Deitz's neck, her husband and children were beside her. The eight- and ten-year-old girls, unable to contain their excitement, were jumping up and down.

"Aren't you proud of your mommy?" the Commodore asked.

"We did all the work," Fredericka yelped. "Mommy likes to sleep late. Daddy has to bring her coffee every morning or she can't open her eyes."

Eldona grabbed her daughter by the elbow and smiled at the Commodore. "Fredericka is our little jokester. Aren't you, dear?"

Fredericka shrugged. "I don't know," she muttered.

Finally the Commodore called up the ten Santas, two of whom were without costumes. "A little mix-up," the Commodore explained to the crowd, "but all of these ten wonderful men will be running around the ship in these Santa suits for the next four days."

"God help us," Luke said under his breath.

As the Commodore put the medal around Bobby Grimes's neck, an obviously inebriated Grimes grabbed the microphone. "I should be wearing a Santa suit right now," he growled. "But there's a thief on board this ship. *Watch out everybody!* Anybody who would bother to steal two of these crummy outfits will have a field day with your cash and jewelry!"

# 13

$\mathbf{H}$arry Crater had scheduled a phone call to his cohorts for seven P.M., but the satellite transmission on his cell phone was not working. With increasing irritability, he waited in his stateroom for an hour, trying to put the call through at ten-minute intervals. At eight o'clock there was a knock at the door. It was Gil Gephardt, the ship's physician, who had taken it upon himself to check up on Crater.

Crater realized too late that without the oversized jacket, he didn't look all that puny. He tried to slump as he stood looking down at his small-framed, owl-like visitor.

"Oh, Mr. Crater, we met briefly when you boarded the ship. I'm Dr. Gephardt. When I noticed you weren't at the cocktail party, I was afraid you had taken ill."

Mind your own business, Crater thought. "I didn't expect to nap so long," he explained. "All the excitement of getting ready for this cruise made my heart pound. I was exhausted." He was aware that Gephardt was studying him closely, his eyes barely blinking.

"Mr. Crater, in my medical opinion, I must say that you look better already. Only a few hours of beneficial sea air and the difference is already remarkable. I'm sure we'll have no need to send for that helicopter at all. Now may I suggest you go downstairs and get yourself some nourishment?"

"I'll be there in a few moments," Crater promised, ignoring the urge to slam the door in Gephardt's face. Instead, he closed it quietly and rushed to the mirror. The grayish paste he had applied to his face before boarding the ship had pretty much worn off. He applied more but was afraid to use as much as he wanted. That doctor was sharper than he looked.

Before he left his room, he made one more attempt to reach his fellow conspirators. This time the call went through. He confirmed the plan. At one A.M. tomorrow night, he would fake a medical emergency. Gephardt would ask the captain to send for the helicopter. A reasonable time for it to arrive would be before daybreak. At that hour, most of the passengers and crew would be asleep. It would be like taking candy from a baby.

When he hung up the phone, Crater headed

out the door. As he hurried down the deserted corridor, he took grim satisfaction in realizing that in thirty-three hours his mission would be accomplished and his big payoff on the way.

He took the elevator to the lounge. Remembering to limp and lean on his cane, he walked across the deserted area, unaware of the boozy outburst from a frustrated Santa that had sent waves of excitement through the cocktail party.

At the door of the dining salon, the maître d' rushed to greet him. "You must be Mr. Crater," he said, placing a supporting arm under Crater's elbow. "We have a wonderful table for you. Dudley has placed you with a remarkable family. Two special youngsters are so excited to be your little helpers on this cruise."

Crater, who had no patience for anyone under thirty, was horrified. As he approached his table, he saw that the one empty chair was between the two little "darlings" he had found intensely irritating at the welcoming ceremony.

As he sat down, Fredericka jumped up. "Can I help you cut your meat?"

Not to be outdone, Gwendolyn threw her arms around his neck. "I love you, Uncle Harry."

Oh my God, he thought, she's going to smear my gray face paint.

# 14

As Ivy Pickering found her place at one of the Readers and Writers tables, she was tingling with the excitement of knowing that there was a thief in their midst. She loved to read mysteries, but to be in the middle of a real life mystery was unbelievable good fortune. She was bursting to report it all to her mother in an e-mail before she went to sleep.

A lively discussion about the missing Santa suits began. The waiter had to struggle to complete taking their orders.

"Are you sure you didn't arrange this, Ivy?" Maggie Quirk, Ivy's roommate joked. "You wanted to stage a murder mystery on board, but it was just too complicated. Besides, it isn't our place. We're *guests* here." Maggie's hazel eyes twinkled. A comfortable size twelve, her short auburn hair fell into waves around her pleasant face. Her lips curved up into a ready smile. There was a certain wryness in her tone, which she'd acquired after the failure of her "perfect" marriage. Three years ago, on her fiftieth birthday, the big surprise had been that her husband told her he wanted a divorce because he needed more excitement in his life. After the shock wore off, Maggie realized it was the best birthday gift she had ever received. "That lump has been boring me for the past ten years," she laughingly told her friends, "and I'm the one who gets dumped." An assistant bank manager, Maggie had resolved to make the most of her free time from that moment on. She had joined the Readers and Writers group and was now delighted to come on the cruise.

"Maggie, we don't need a murder mystery," Ivy responded. "Wouldn't it be fun to try and figure out who would take those Santa Claus suits and why?"

"That poor cruise director looks a little confused. There were probably only eight suits to start with," Tommy Lawton, the vice president of the group, commented as he dug into his smoked salmon.

I believe two suits *were* stolen, Ivy thought, and I'm going to make it my business to find out what happened. Then I'll really have an excuse to spend time with the Reillys and the Meehans.

Everyone agreed that the appetizers and the

entrées they'd ordered were delicious. "This food is surprisingly good," Maggie commented, as the entrées were being cleared. "And it tastes even better because it's free."

The waiter began serving salads.

Lawton looked perplexed. "Did you forget to pass these around before the main course?"

"No, sir," the man sniffed. "This is the way they do it in Paris."

"Never been there," Lawton said cheerfully. "Maybe if I win the lottery."

Ivy knew that if she had salad she'd never have room for dessert. Pushing back her chair, she playfully whispered, "Don't say anything interesting till I get back." As she exited the dining salon, she made a point of waving to the Santas who were seated at the tables along her path. She knew that one of them would be sitting at her table the next night. She couldn't wait. She hoped it would be Bobby Grimes, the one who had told everybody to watch their wallets. Unless of course the Commodore banned him from wearing a Santa outfit. They'd given Grimes the hook after his outburst.

After visiting the ladies' room, Ivy decided to take a quick detour to the Chapel of Repose. It would be nice to include a description of the room in the e-mail she'd send to her mother tonight. No one would be there now, and she'd get a chance to get a good look around in peace and quiet.

"This stupid suit makes me itch," Bull's-Eye complained. "I've got to take it off or I'll go nuts."

They'd been sitting in the dark behind the altar, complaining to each other about how hungry they were.

"Then do it," Highbridge snapped.

Bull's-Eye stood up, removed the jacket and pants, and dropped them on the floor. Clad only in his boxer shorts, he began to stretch his arms and jump up and down. At that precise moment, the door of the chapel opened and the light was flicked on.

For an instant, Bull's-Eye and Ivy stared at each other.

"Aaaaahhhhhhhhhhhh!" Ivy screamed.

Before Bull's-Eye could move, Ivy was out the door, her feet flying along the corridor and down the stairs, continuing to shriek as she made her way back to the others.

"Now you've done it," Highbridge said frantically, pulling on his beard and stocking cap. "Get dressed. We've got to get out of here."

Back in the dining salon, the Santa Cruisers were in for their second shock of the evening.

Heads swiveled at the sounds emanating from the approaching Ivy. When she appeared in the doorway, she cried out, "I saw Left Hook Louie's ghost! He's in the Chapel of Repose getting ready for another fight! *He's with us on the cruise!!!*"

There was an instant of silence and then the tables with the Oklahoma Readers and Writers burst into laughter. "That's our Ivy!" one of them shouted.

The amusement spread to the other tables.

"I mean it," Ivy protested. "He's in the chapel. Come see!"

With one exception, everyone in the dining room continued to chuckle.

Eric jumped up and turned to the Commodore. "I'll check it out, sir."

The Commodore grabbed Eric's sleeve and pulled him back into his seat. "Don't be ridiculous. The woman's a loon. Now enjoy your dessert."

# 15

$B$ull's-Eye and Highbridge ran out of the
chapel, and down the corridor to the nearest
companionway. The bells on their stocking caps
tinkled as their feet, barely touching the steps, de-
scended to the next level. Two flights below they
found an outside door, pushed it open, and
stepped out onto a large deserted deck lined with
beach chairs. It was immediately obvious that
there was no place to hide. They hurried toward
the ship's stern, up a set of wrought-iron steps,
and found themselves on the pool deck. A bar was
at one end. A wall of glass windows at the other
end of the deck looked into a cafeteria-style dining room marked "The Lido" where several waiters were carrying platters and placing them on a
long table.

"They must be setting up for the midnight buffet," Highbridge whispered. "People do nothing
but eat on these cruise ships."

"Except us," Bull's-Eye grunted. "Let's go in and get some food."

"You've got to be kidding," Highbridge objected.

"An empty stomach is nothing to kid about. Just stay calm. Act hungry. Follow me."

They strolled past the pool, through the double doors, and headed for the buffet table. An ice sculpture of Marlon Brando in a naval uniform, his feet in a drip pan, served as the somewhat-watery centerpiece.

"Sorry, the midnight buffet doesn't start until eleven," a waiter on his way to the kitchen stopped to tell them.

"Yeah, well we just got back from the North Pole, and it's too late to have dinner downstairs," Bull's-Eye explained, his voice trying to sound jolly. Even to his own ears the words didn't ring true, so he started to laugh. He realized the laugh didn't ring true either.

"We'll grab enough to tide us and the reindeer over," Highbridge added. "Rudolph gets temperamental when he hasn't eaten."

The waiter shrugged. "None of the hot food is out yet. I hope Rudolph likes cheese."

Bull's-Eye nodded, then whispered under his breath. "Enough with the small talk. We'll sneak in later. Let's grab whatever they have and get out of here fast."

# 16

*Doesn't anybody believe me?"* Ivy screamed.

As one, the Oklahoma Readers and Writers group yelled, "No!"

At the Reilly-Meehan table, the three couples exchanged worried glances.

"I've been to a lot of murder mystery weekends," Nora said, "but no one ever sounded as convincing as Ivy. I don't think this is an act."

"She definitely believes she saw something," Regan agreed.

Dudley was sitting nearby. He jumped up and ran to Ivy. "Miss Pickering, I know you're trying to have some fun on this cruise but . . ."

Ignoring Dudley, Ivy ran to Alvirah's table. "They all think I'm joking. I'm not. I saw Left Hook Louie in tartan plaid boxer shorts in the chapel. He was warming up for a fight. Like this . . ." She started jumping up and down and stretching her arms.

With a regretful glance at her as yet untouched

crème brulée, Alvirah hoisted herself out of the chair. "Let's go take a look," she said.

"We'll all go with you, Miss Pickering," Jack said decisively.

"Thank you. Call me Ivy."

Not wanting to wait for an elevator, they took the companionway up to the Boat Deck. Nora tucked a reassuring hand under Ivy's elbow as they started down the corridor to the Chapel of Repose. She's trembling, Nora realized. She's *really* scared.

"I just wanted to take a peek at the chapel because I'm sending an e-mail to my mother . . . I don't care how good it is for you, I hate salad. Besides, they didn't serve the salad on time. I thought I'd take a few minutes to check out the chapel while everyone was chomping on their rabbit food. Maybe even say a prayer for my mother. She's eighty-five, but still going strong. Sharp as a tack. She took up yoga. It's been wonderful for her. She goes to church every day. That's why I knew she'd be interested in what the chapel here was like. . . ."

"The chapel is very special to the Commodore," Dudley said quickly. "He was hoping someone would decide to get married on this cruise. The chapel is perfect for *any* special occasion. . . ."

Jack pulled open the ornate chapel door. The sanctuary was in darkness except for the faint glow of the outside lights filtering through the stained-glass windows. "Ivy, was the light on when you got here?"

"No. I pulled open the door and saw the switch right away. It has a glow. I flicked it on and . . . ohhhhhhhhh. But I did *not* turn it off when I left!" she added positively.

"We plan to encourage our guests to turn out lights whenever possible. It's so wasteful to leave on your cabin lights when you go to dinner. The Commodore is very concerned about global warming," Dudley explained, then realized that no one was paying attention to him.

Jack reached over and flicked the switch. The overhead and side lights went on, illuminating the chapel. Ivy pointed to the side of the altar. "That's where he was jumping and stretching. Left Hook Louie! I know it sounds crazy, but he was here. Or at least his ghost was here."

"Ivy, did he *say* anything to you?" Alvirah asked. "I'm sure he wouldn't have wanted to scare you like this. After all, you're honoring him on this trip."

"No. He just stared at me. The boxes with a special classic edition of his first book, *Planter's Punch*, never made it on board. Maybe that upset him."

*"Planter's Punch?"* Regan asked.

"Yes. Left Hook Louie's boxer-turned-detective was named Pug Planter. That first book was a huge bestseller. But as I said, the classic edition we were supposed to sell on board never made it to the ship on time."

Nora rolled her eyes. "I know all about books not arriving where I have an appearance scheduled."

"The books didn't arrive, but Left Hook Louie certainly made an appearance!" Ivy insisted. "I know it has to have been a ghost. But I always thought you could see through a ghost. And he was making a lot of noise when he was jumping up and down."

"You say he was next to the altar?" Jack asked as he walked up the aisle.

"Yes. He was right there." Ivy pointed, following Jack.

Regan noticed that the heavy damask cloth covering the altar was askew. She picked up one corner and looked underneath it. There was nothing there.

Alvirah glanced under it, too, and, always the cleaning woman, smoothed and straightened the altar cloth.

"I know what you're all thinking," Ivy said. "That I imagined this whole thing. But I'm telling you I saw a man in boxer shorts. If it wasn't Left Hook Louie, it was his twin."

"Ivy, did anyone in your Readers and Writers group know you were coming up here?" Regan asked.

"No. I didn't know I was coming myself."

"It doesn't look as though Louie left anything behind," Jack observed.

Ivy cast a quick suspicious glance at Jack to see if he was being sarcastic.

"Someone might have been planning a practical joke," Jack theorized. "Perhaps you caught him practicing up here. Do you know everyone in your group?"

"Some I know better than others. A couple of the husbands I've only met a few times. But *none* of them look like Left Hook Louie."

"You have posters of Louie all over the ship. Maybe someone on board is planning to surprise your group at one of your seminars," Alvirah suggested. "Naturally you were so frightened when you saw him that you only had the quickest of glances, then turned and ran."

"I know what I saw," Ivy insisted. "I saw someone who was a dead ringer for Left Hook Louie."

Luke had been standing by the last pew. Something on the floor just inside the pew caught his eye. He leaned over and picked up a small metallic ball with slits and a smaller solid ball on the inside.

"What have you got there?" Nora inquired.

"Got where?" Alvirah asked, her ears always capable of hearing a whispered conversation three rooms away.

Luke walked forward and held out his hand. "It's probably nothing. Unless Left Hook Louie had this sewn to his boxer shorts."

Alvirah took the tiny ball and shook it. It made a tinkling noise. "They use these all over for Christmas decorations." She smiled. "We'll keep it as evidence."

Dudley's heart nearly stopped. He knew that that little bell had come off one of the Santa Claus caps. Could it have been from one of the stolen caps?

With a last look around, Regan turned to Ivy. "You look as though you need to relax. Would you like to have a nightcap with us?"

"I'd love to!" Ivy replied enthusiastically. "Maybe the Readers and Writers group isn't on my side, but you all are, and I couldn't be happier."

"We'll figure out what's happening on this ship," Alvirah promised heartily.

Dudley wanted to cry. The only reason for this cruise was to generate good publicity for the *Royal*

*Mermaid.* To let the world know what a wonderful ship it was and how perfect cruising on the *Mermaid* would be, to encourage people to open their wallets and hop on board. Now with these busy-bodies the whole thing could turn into a public relations nightmare. The first commercial sailing of the *Royal Mermaid* would resemble a ghost ship.

Dudley couldn't let that happen.

He just couldn't.

# 17

Commodore Weed was holding court at his table recounting the story of how he had decided to change his life by refurbishing the *Royal Mermaid* and spending the rest of his days sailing around the globe. "My love for the sea began when I received a plastic boat at age five. I had my little life vest on and my father pulled me around the lake near our house. . . ."

Eric and Dr. Gephardt had heard this story at least a hundred times. They were required to sit at the Commodore's table each evening and be charming to the rotating guests. Tonight the Jaspers, an elderly couple who'd bid on the cruise at a fundraiser for Save the Amphibians, and the Snyders, a middle-aged couple from the Readers and Writers group, had the privilege of dining with the ship's officers.

Eric was desperate to get away, frantically wondering what course of action his two felons had taken after being discovered in the chapel. Why did Bull's-Eye take off his Santa outfit, and what was he doing jumping up and down? Had he gone crazy? Had the Reillys and Meehans gone up to the chapel with that screaming dingbat? He'd seen them leave the dining room together. Bull's-Eye and Highbridge couldn't have been stupid enough to stay in the chapel. Or could they?

Eric was furious that Dudley had managed to escape from the table when Ivy Pickering went nuts.

Dr. Gephardt had circulated at the cocktail party before going up to check on Harry Crater. Crater must have given a lot of money to charity, Gephardt thought, for the Commodore to have risked having someone on board who was so sick. He glanced over at the table where he knew Crater was sitting and saw the old man getting out of his chair. The children on either side of Crater jumped up eagerly.

Crater was about to go out of his mind. The kids had driven him crazy all during dinner and their parents' conversation was mind-numbing. At least the outburst from that woman had provided a much-needed jolt to his system.

"Mr. Crater, I must get a picture of you with the girls," Eldona insisted. "We'll make a scrapbook of the cruise and send it to you. We'll have to get your address. Please sit back down."

Crater begrudgingly agreed and began his descent. Eldona's eyes widened in horror as she realized Gwendolyn had pulled Crater's chair away from the table, just as she had been taught in the Assisting Senior Citizens etiquette class. Eldona watched as the expression on Crater's face turned to bewilderment and then panic when he realized there was no chair to catch him. A loud thump sounded as Crater disappeared below the table.

Gasps from surrounding diners interrupted the Commodore's tale of the happy years he had spent at sailing camp on Cape Cod.

Cursing under his breath, sprawled flat on his back, and momentarily shocked, Crater knew that he'd thrown out his back again. Fredericka leaned over, having dunked her napkin in her water glass, and began wiping his face. "There, there," she cooed. "It was Mommy's fault. Ewww, what's this gray stuff on your face?"

Crater grabbed the napkin from her hand. "My medicine causes that," he growled. "Get your hands off me."

By now Dr. Gephardt was squatting beside him, thrilled that he had a reason to flee the Commodore's table. Gephardt held up a finger. "Mr. Crater can you see my finger?"

Crater slapped the doctor's hand away and attempted to get up. But the pain in his back made it impossible to move.

Gephardt frowned. "We're getting a stretcher. We can't take any chances with a man in your condition. What exactly is wrong with you?"

"At the moment, everything!"

"Can you move your legs?"

"I have a bad back. I twisted it. It's happened before. I'll be fine. Just help me up."

Gephardt shook his head solemnly. "No, no. That was a hard fall, and we can't be sure that you haven't injured yourself seriously. As a trained medical practitioner, I insist that you spend the night in the infirmary. If necessary, we will summon your helicopter."

*"No!"* Crater exploded as he pushed himself on one elbow, wincing as he felt the old familiar spasms in his back send shooting pain throughout his body. "I don't want to leave this Santa Cruise. I earned this trip by giving loads of money to charity."

Fredericka and Gwendolyn jumped up and down, clapping their hands. "Yayyyyyyyyyy. We'll visit you in the ship's hospital."

Two infirmary attendants arrived with a stretcher. Crater felt himself being carefully lifted onto it and then felt straps being tied around his arms to secure him to it. As they started to carry him out of the dining room, he heard the doctor say to one of the medics, "I have the number of his helicopter. Perhaps I should call and warn them that they might have to come pick up Mr. Crater at any time."

# 18

The Sports Deck of the *Royal Mermaid* was at the ship's stern. In addition to the infamous rock-climbing wall, there was a basketball court and a miniature golf course. Bull's-Eye and Highbridge had carried their trays, on which they'd haphazardly gathered cheese, crackers, and grapes, from the Lido buffet, looking for a place to hide and eat. When they discovered the sports area, Highbridge pointed to a miniature red barn hovering over the seventh hole of the golf course. An open-mouthed cow was leaning out the window over the barn door, the gap between its teeth obviously the target for golfers. Once someone hit a ball through the cow's choppers, the ball would hopefully have enough momentum to roll through the barn, down a crevice, and land in putting distance of the hole.

"Let's hide behind the barn," Highbridge suggested. "This is the back of the ship, so no one will see us from the other direction. And the golf course is closed now."

"My cards!" Bull's-Eye cried suddenly.

"What?"

"Being around these games made me think of my cards! I left them in that other room."

"So what?"

"I've got to get them back. They're important!"

The two men could hear the sound of voices coming up the companionway. "Come on!" Highbridge said impatiently.

With swift steps they walked around the fenced-in basketball court and made their way along the intricately designed golf course, until they were safely behind the façade of the barn. They sat with their backs against the barn and glumly wolfed down the cheese.

The night was becoming overcast.

"We're moving along pretty fast," Highbridge observed, staring out at the churning white wake cutting through the vast expanse of black water. "But I don't like that sky."

"Why not? You want stars and a full moon so that we can't be missed?"

"I had a yacht until the Feds got nasty. I know this kind of weather. We're in for a big storm."

# 19

Despite the many interruptions, the Commodore was determined to finish the saga of his seafaring life. And by golly he did. The two couples who were sitting at the table had managed to keep smiles fixed on their faces during his gasket-by-gasket description of the *Royal Mermaid,* now the fastest ship of its kind on the seas.

As the Commodore patted his mouth with his napkin and placed it on the table, Eric leapt up. "Have a wonderful evening, everyone," he said. "I'll see to Mr. Crater and then mingle with our other guests."

"Give me a hug," the Commodore said, his arms outstretched.

Eric leaned down and allowed his uncle to practically smother him in an embrace topped off with a kiss on the cheek.

"He's the son I never had," the Commodore explained to his stultified guests, who now resembled wax figures.

As he left the dining room, Eric saw the Meehans and Reillys, accompanied by that idiot Dudley and the screamer, coming down the companionway. He felt a momentary sense of relief. Obviously they had *not* run into Bull's-Eye and the Bean Counter. Now the appropriate thing for him to do was to ask if everything was all right.

With an air of superiority, Dudley said dismissively, "Don't worry, Eric. I have everything under control. It's possible we have a practical joker in our midst who unfortunately frightened Miss Pickering. I'm sure he will reveal himself in the next day or so."

"We're on our way for a nightcap," Ivy said coquettishly. "Would you like to join us?"

"Thank you, but I have to check on one of our guests who's in the infirmary."

"Already?" Alvirah asked.

"Unfortunately, yes. Perhaps you've noticed him. Mr. Crater, the man with the cane. He was at the table with the Dietz children. . . ."

"Poor guy," Luke murmured.

Eric smiled and rolled his eyes, turning on the charm, which he knew he was so capable of demonstrating. "You put him at the table with those pesky kids, right, Dudley?" he asked playfully, tapping him on the arm.

"I worked very hard on the seating arrangements," Dudley said defensively. "Those children are with us because of their caring, loving natures that their mother captured in her beautiful and heartwarming Christmas letter."

"Well, one of the girls was so caring, she yanked the chair out from under Crater and he fell backward when he tried to sit down. That's why he was carried out of the dining room strapped to a stretcher."

"We missed all that?" Ivy asked, dismayed.

"I'm afraid so," Eric answered.

"Well, that's all right," Ivy decided. "I now have these wonderful people on my side, helping me to get to the bottom of things." She pointed to Jack. "How many people have the head of the Major Case Squad of New York City working with them?" She then pointed to the others. "How many people have a renowned private investigator, a famous suspense writer, and a prize-winning amateur sleuth taking the time to dig for the truth? *Not many,* I tell you! But Ivy Pickering is proud to say, 'I have them all.' "

By now Eric's mouth was wide open. He had met the couples earlier, when he'd been forced to give up his room to the Meehans, but he had no idea that Alvirah's guests included the head of the Major Case Squad of New York City. Eric was worried—Bull's-Eye looked exactly like the ex-fighter who became a famous writer. The news headlines announced that Bull's-Eye was missing, and his picture was all over the media. Would Jack Reilly have any suspicions that the man Pickering had seen was not a dead writer, but an escaped criminal? Thank God Ivy said the ghost was jumping up and down in boxing shorts. Eric hoped Jack Reilly would not make the connection. For an awful moment, Eric had a vision of himself in a prison cell with no window, never mind a balcony. He had to find Bull's-Eye and the Bean Counter before somebody else spotted them. He knew they couldn't be in the chapel but he wanted to check it out anyway, then he'd work his way through the ship.

Eric forced himself to smile. "Well, we can all feel safe with such impressive law enforcement figures on board," he said heartily. "Now, if you'll excuse me . . ." He started past them up the companionway.

He's not going to see Mr. Crater, Dudley realized. The ship's infirmary is on the lowest deck. What's he up to?

In the next ten minutes, Eric raced through the chapel, looked into his uncle's suite—even though the door was locked and no one would have been able to get in—and checked out all the hiding places that he could possibly imagine. Large as the *Royal Mermaid* was, there weren't many spots to hide. Whenever Eric spotted a Santa, he rushed over to him only to be disappointed. They've got to be starving by now, he told himself. Was there any chance they'd risk going to get something to eat?

Eric looked at his watch and realized that the buffet wouldn't be open yet. I'd better go down and check on Crater, he thought, and then I'll head to the Lido.

# 20

Nora and Luke begged off joining the group in the piano lounge.

"We got in late last night and were up so early this morning," Nora pleaded. "We'll see you guys at breakfast."

Willy yawned. "Alvirah, you've got enough stamina for everyone on the ship. Do you mind if I turn in, too?"

Ivy, whose heart had begun to sink at the prospect of losing her intimate visit with the celebrities, perked up when Alvirah said, "Go ahead, Willy. I won't be long."

"I'll find a nice quiet table for us," Dudley promised.

At the entrance to the lounge, Ivy spotted a couple sitting at a window table. "Oh, there's my roommate, Maggie," Ivy exclaimed as she looked across the room. "Who's the Santa Claus with her?"

"I can't tell from here," Dudley said. "But I think it's Ted Cannon. He's one of the taller Santas."

"Would you like to invite them to join us?" Regan asked Ivy.

"No," Ivy answered decisively. She was really fond of Maggie, but her friend had been laughing just as hard as everybody else when she told them that she had seen Left Hook Louie. Besides, she wanted a chance to talk to Regan, Jack, and Alvirah with as few others around as possible. She didn't mind Dudley so much—the poor guy just looked worn out.

Dudley led the way to a corner table. He gestured grandly to Alvirah, "Ms. Meehan, where would you like to sit?"

"Never with my back to the door," Alvirah joked. "I don't want to miss a thing."

"Neither does anyone else in this group," Regan murmured. She always teased Jack that the only disadvantage of being with him was that he could never sit facing the wall because of his job. This meant that if they couldn't find a banquette and sit side by side, Regan's view would be solely of Jack, which, as he pointed out, "was treat enough for anyone."

"Dudley, how about if you sit next to me?" Alvirah suggested. "Whew," she said, grabbing onto a chair. "The sea must be getting choppy."

"The sea is an unpredictable lady," Dudley said knowingly, helping Alvirah ease into a chair. "As are most ladies," he added with a raised eyebrow. "We men never know what to expect. Isn't that right, Jack?"

Regan was amused at the expression on Jack's face. She knew it must have aggravated him when Dudley insinuated they were birds of a feather. Jack had already told her that he thought Dudley was a harmless bumbler.

Alvirah was regretting the fact that she had not worn her sunburst pin with the hidden microphone. It had often picked up something someone had said that turned out to be revealing when she listened quietly to the replay.

As soon as everyone was seated, a waiter materialized and took their orders.

Alvirah turned to Dudley. "You've had quite a day, haven't you?" she asked sympathetically. "Any news on that waiter who took a swan dive into the Port of Miami?"

Dudley felt a faint fluttering in his stomach. He hadn't had the courage to go to his office and read his e-mail. He was grateful for the fact that most of the time local TV stations weren't picked up by the ship's communications system. He knew that the Commodore's business office in Miami had probably contacted him about any coverage of the incident that had broken on the evening news. I'm like Scarlett O'Hara, he admitted to himself ruefully, I'll think about it tomorrow. He was able to answer Alvirah honestly, "I haven't heard anything else. As the Commodore announced, his offense was of a domestic nature. The man was *way* overdue on his alimony."

Ivy wagged her finger. "That's one good thing about never meeting the right person. I've never had to worry about a deadbeat ex. When I was little, Papa gave his paycheck unopened to my mother every Friday night, and she handed him his allowance. It worked just fine until he asked for a raise." She smiled at the waiter as he placed an apple martini in front of her. With great anticipation, she took a sip. "The things they can do with apples . . ." she exulted. "Oh, I should have waited until you were all served. I'm so wound up, but I feel safe with all of you." As soon as everyone had their drinks, she held up her glass. "Let's have a toast!"

"Cheers," they chorused as rain suddenly began beating noisily against the windows.

"I wouldn't want to be out there," Regan com-

114

mented as the ship suddenly rolled from side to side. *"Listen* to that wind! It's starting to howl. This storm moved in pretty fast, didn't it, Dudley?"

"As I said, the sea is an unpredictable lady," Dudley pronounced as he clutched his glass. "I've been through many such storms that have caught us by surprise. If this is like most others, it will go as fast as it came. And that's what I predict."

"As long as there are no icebergs out there," Ivy said cheerfully. "I've had enough surprises for tonight. Well, here comes Benedict Arnold."

"What?" Regan asked, puzzled.

"My roommate, Maggie."

Maggie Quirk was crossing the room toward them, followed by Ted Cannon, who had removed his beard and cap. "Whoa!" Maggie cried as the ship suddenly lurched again. She grabbed Ted's arm.

"The ship didn't roll, Maggie!" Ivy called out sweetly. "You just imagined it!"

Maggie smiled as she approached the table. "Ivy, I'm sorry. At first, we all thought you staged that scene because you wanted so much to have a murder mystery on board. Now everyone knows that something *really* frightened you."

"There certainly is something going on," Jack agreed, as he and Dudley stood. Introductions were made and extra chairs pulled up to the table.

"Ted knows I'm your roommate, so he asked me about you," Maggie explained.

Alvirah noticed the cap in Ted's hands. "That's where it came from!" she exclaimed.

"Where *what* came from?" Regan asked.

Alvirah fished in her pocket. "The little bell we found in the chapel. It's the same as the two on the tip of Ted's cap." She turned to Dudley. "How many bells are supposed to be on those caps?"

Dudley hesitated. "Two."

"Dudley," Alvirah said, "we should check the eight caps the Santas are wearing and see if they all still have two bells. If they do, then it looks as if someone who had one of the stolen Santa suits was in the chapel."

Regan stared at Dudley. He would certainly have recognized the bell as coming from one of the caps. He hadn't mentioned it before. Clearly, he doesn't want us to think that the person or persons who stole those outfits is wandering around the ship in them. And if that were the case, were they somehow connected to whatever it was that Ivy saw?

Another rolling motion of the ship knocked their glasses over.

"Time to call it a night," Jack said as they all pushed back from the dripping table. "Be careful, everybody. This storm feels as though it's getting worse."

Trying to be cheerful, Dudley proclaimed, "Don't worry, everyone. You're snug as a bug in a rug in this old tub."

The psychic's warning flashed into Alvirah's mind. *"I see a tub. A large tub. You are not safe in it. . . ."*

# 21

"This is nuts!" Bull's-Eye spat out the words as he and Highbridge huddled behind the barn, driving rain hitting them from every direction. "We're getting soaked. When it gets light, what are we going to do? Even if it's stopped raining, we're gonna look like a couple of drowned rats. There's *no way* we'll be able to walk around in these Santa suits."

Highbridge longed for his Greenwich estate with the wonderful bubbling Jacuzzi in the master bathroom and its view of Long Island Sound. I had so much family money I didn't even *need* to cheat investors, he thought. But it had been so much fun. Now, as he sat miserable and wet, wearing a scratchy Santa suit, he realized he should have gone into therapy and worked out his criminal instincts. And all the money he had wasted on his gold-digging ex-girlfriend who was now schussing down the slopes of Aspen with someone else.

If he didn't get to Fishbowl Island there was one thing he could count on—she'd never qualify for a cruise like this by visiting him in the clink. The thought of trading his Armani wardrobe for an orange jumpsuit riddled him with even more anxiety, if that was possible.

"Eric's got to be looking for us," Highbridge said. "It's his neck, too, if we're found."

Suddenly the blades of a windmill on the ninth hole, which had been spinning wildly, came loose and went flying through the air. They landed inches from their sandaled feet.

# 22

Eric knew that if he ran into Alvirah Meehan on an isolated deck, he'd toss her overboard. If it weren't for her, Bull's-Eye and Highbridge would still be safely in his stateroom, and he'd be that much closer to his big payoff. The way things were, they had told Eric they wouldn't give him the second half of his money when their people picked them up off Fishbowl Island. And he'd be lucky if one or the other of them, once they were safely outside the United States, didn't write a letter explaining to the authorities exactly how they fled the country.

Eric had another thought. If he came across Dudley on an isolated deck, it would be an even greater pleasure to throw him in the drink. All this was coursing through his mind, as he was temporarily forced to abandon the search for his two charges and check on Crater. Grabbing on to the bannister, he hurried down flight after flight of steps to the medical facility in the bowels of the ship. With each descending flight, the rocking of the ship lessened somewhat, but even so he had to steady himself along the guardrail of the passageway outside the infirmary.

Expecting to find an empty waiting room, Eric was disagreeably surprised to find it filled with queasy passengers demanding ear patches for their seasickness. Bobby Grimes, whose drunken outburst had been the talk of the cocktail party, was holding his head in his hands. When he spotted Eric, he barked, "I knew I should have stayed home."

I wish you had, too, Eric thought, as he crossed the small reception area and opened the door that led to Gephardt's office and the treatment rooms. The nurse behind the desk was sorting medication. She had the aura of a guard dog. Looking at Eric, she frowned in disapproval.

"My uncle wants me to speak to Crater," he told her. "Which room is he in?"

"Second on the right," she answered crisply. "Dr. Gephardt is with him."

The door to Crater's room was open. Gephardt was beside the bed. Eric heard him say, "This shot will definitely relieve those back spasms, Mr. Crater. It should also help you sleep."

"I want to go back to my room," Crater protested, his voice drowsy.

"Not tonight," Gephardt said firmly. "Your back is bad, and we're in a storm. The last thing we need is for you to fall again. Down here you're in the calmest part of the ship, and we can keep an eye on you."

Crater tried to sit up but fell back immediately, moaning in pain.

"See what I mean!" Gephardt said triumphantly. "The medicine will start to work in a few minutes. Now just relax."

Eric tapped the door to announce his presence and walked over to the bed. "Mr. Crater, we're so sorry about your accident. But you're in good hands with Dr. Gephardt."

"Those miserable kids," Crater moaned. "Who stuck me at that table?"

"Never mind," Eric said soothingly. "From now on you'll be seated at the Commodore's table. He's wonderfully entertaining."

"That's right," Gephardt agreed. "Mr. Crater, you said yourself these back spasms don't last long. We hope to have you up and about as soon as possible. But you absolutely *cannot* move now. Of course, we can always summon your helicopter when the storm passes, if you feel you'd be more comfortable at home."

Crater's face darkened. "Where's my cell phone?" he asked as he drifted off to sleep.

Gephardt nodded to Eric, indicating they should step outside. Eric followed him into his office. A lightbulb had gone off in Eric's head.

"He seems alone," Eric said solicitously. "Is he traveling with anyone?"

"No," Gephardt answered slowly. "He really puzzles me. His back is certainly in spasm, but he's not as sickly as he appeared. His body is surprisingly muscular and all his vital signs are perfect. I can't understand why he was wearing a grayish makeup on his face. Underneath it, his skin is ruddy, but that stuff makes him look like a cadaver."

Eric glanced down at Gephardt's desk. Crater's chart was right there, his cabin number next to his name. "You're definitely keeping him here overnight?" Eric asked.

Gephardt nodded solemnly. "At least overnight. I know he'd prefer to be back in his own room, but with that shot I gave him he'll be lights out until tomorrow morning." He then smiled. "Can you believe the Deitz children's mother already had them make Get Well cards for him? He tore them up unopened."

Eric laughed, pretending to share a moment with Gephardt.

"Now, Eric, if you'll excuse me, I have a waiting room full of patients," Gephardt said briskly.

For a split second Eric was angry at being dismissed by a nerd like Gephardt when he was dying to get out of there anyway. But the anger passed quickly. Now at least he had a plan.

Moving even faster than before, he hurried back up the companionway to the Lido. It was nearly empty. "Not too many takers for the buffet tonight?" he asked one of the waiters.

"Not with this weather."

"I thought I'd see some of the Santas up here," Eric said, trying to sound casual. "So many people were talking to them at dinner, they didn't get much chance to eat."

"Two of them came up here really early. We weren't even set up yet. They took some grapes and cheese."

Eric's pulse quickened. That had to have been Bull's-Eye and Highbridge. "Did they sit in here?"

"No, they took the food with them and went out the back." The waiter turned his attention to the buffet table. "We're starting to put everything away early. Can I get you anything?"

"No, thanks," Eric answered quickly. "See you around." He knew the waiter would think he was insane if he went out the back door into the rain. Instead, he took the inside archway that led to the bank of elevators, strode past them, and exited through a side door that opened onto the deck. A driving rain immediately soaked his uniform. Getting on his hands and knees so the waiters wouldn't see him walking around in the rain like a lunatic, he headed toward the back of the ship. If Bull's-Eye and Highbridge were hiding out there, he'd have to let them know he was in the vicinity.

He waited until he got to the sports area before he started singing, "Santa Claus is comin' to town."

# 23

Regan and Jack escorted Alvirah back to her room.

"Get right to bed, Alvirah," Jack said. "The way this ship is rocking, it would be very easy to fall."

"Don't worry about me," Alvirah said. "For forty years I stood on wobbly tables to dust chandeliers. I always said I could have been a tightrope walker."

Regan laughed and gave Alvirah a peck on the cheek. "Take Jack's advice. We'll see you in the morning."

Alvirah let herself into the room and was comforted by the sight of an almost invisible Willy wrapped up in the blankets and the sound of his rumbling snore. The desk lamp was on. I'm too wound up to sleep, she told herself. And anyhow, I want to record everything that happened today while it's still fresh in my mind. My editor, Charlie, said if I could get an exciting story out of this cruise, he'd be interested, but he didn't want a travelogue or just a feel-good piece. "I appreciate all the good deeds these people have done," he had said, not sounding particularly appreciative, "but it doesn't sell papers."

Well, some pretty interesting things have happened today, Alvirah thought as she retrieved her sunburst pin with the hidden recorder out of the safe and settled down at the desk.

"When we arrived at the ship, they didn't even have a room for us," she began, her voice soft.

"Mmmmmmm." Behind her, she heard Willy stir. Sometimes he could sleep through a fire alarm, but with the way the ship is moving, I might wake him up if I talk in here, she realized. I'll stand outside the door.

In the passageway, Alvirah grasped the railing with one hand and with the other held the sunburst pin close to her lips as she recounted every detail of the day's events. She ran down the list of what had happened: the room mix-up, Dudley's fall from the rock-climbing wall, the waiter jumping overboard, the missing Santa suits, and Ivy spotting a ghost. She paused and added one more detail. "It's funny that Dudley didn't explain immediately where that bell we found in the chapel must have come from. He had to have recognized that it was from one of the Santa caps. That really is something to think about."

Alvirah clicked off her recorder and went back inside the room. In the bathroom, she removed her makeup, brushed her teeth, and changed into a nightgown and robe. She crawled into bed next to Willy and was about to flick off the desk lamp from the bedside switch when she noticed the cards that Willy had been playing with were resting in a furrow of the blanket. She picked up the deck, intending to put it in the night table drawer, when something caught her eye.

"That's funny," she said aloud. The top card was the jack of hearts but there was something unusual about it. What *was* it? Around the head of the jack there was a frame with what looked like an abstract design. Alvirah studied the design closely. Acting on a hunch, she carried the cards into the bathroom and turned on the light. A makeup mirror with a magnifying glass was attached to the wall by the sink. She held the jack of hearts up to the mirror. The seemingly abstract design, as reflected in the mirror, was actually a series of numbers.

"I thought so," she murmured triumphantly as she quickly glanced through the deck. It soon became clear that only the royal cards were marked with the abstract design. She separated the jacks, queens, and kings, and one by one held them up to the mirror. All twelve contained a different series of numbers. What do those numbers stand for and who do the cards belong to? she wondered. When we showed them to Eric, he was so brusque and dismissive I was sure he'd never seen them before.

Hmmm. Alvirah again reviewed the day's events and remembered how Winston was surprised to find potato chips on the floor of Eric's room. Now a mysterious deck of cards was found in his drawer. Had someone *else* been using Eric's room? Could this have been the unofficial break room for some of the workers who were getting the *Royal Mermaid* ready this week? I wouldn't blame them. Next to the Commodore's suite, it's the best accommodation on the ship.

But as Alvirah got into bed, her instinct told her that it wasn't workmen who'd been in the room.

There's something else going on here, she thought, and I'm going to find out what it is.

# 24

Bianca Garcia had been a reporter with a local Miami television station since September. Young, fiery, and ambitious, she was determined to make a name for herself in the industry. So far, she had only been assigned to fluff pieces, most of which were given about thirty seconds of airtime. She had gone to cover the Santa Cruise, expecting a boring afternoon with zip, zero, nothing to report.

But when the waiter jumped ship and Bianca's crew recorded it all on tape, she knew she had the kind of segment that might have legs. When it didn't make the six P.M. broadcast because of a breaking story about an overturned tractor trailer that had spilled its load of dairy products all over the highway and tied up traffic in every direction, Bianca had been chagrined.

But as it turned out—like her grandmother always said—"Sometimes when you get stinkerooed,

God has a reason for it." Good old grandma. At eighty-five, she still was Bianca's best sounding board.

Sure enough, after the six o'clock broadcast, the producer had said, "Bianca, I'm sick of the scrambled-eggs story. I can give you more time on the ten o'clock show."

Bianca had stayed in close touch with her contact at the police department all evening to learn if there was anything more to the swimming waiter than the fact that he was behind on his alimony checks. To her delight there was.

She also spent time researching the history of the cruise ship. In anticipation of reporting what was now a much juicier story than what she had had for the earlier broadcast, at quarter of ten Bianca touched up her makeup and brushed her long dark hair. During the commercial break, she sashayed across the newsroom, climbed up on the stool at the right of the anchor's desk, and crossed her shapely legs.

"Hello, Mary Louise," Bianca said sweetly to the woman who had considered the ten o'clock broadcast "The Mary Louise Show" for the past decade. Bianca intended to occupy her seat before too much longer, then move on to bigger and better things.

Mary Louise was no dummy. She had gotten rid

of other ambitious newcomers, some of whom abandoned the field of journalism after a brief stint at the station. Mary Louise had already begun the process of putting the skids on this annoying snip. Her smile was thin. "Hello, Bianca. I understand you have a cute little cruise ship story for us."

"I'm sure you'll enjoy it," Bianca promised as the producer pointed to Mary Louise, indicating that the commercial break was over.

"It's holiday time," Mary Louise began, "and our gal on the scene, Bianca Garcia, went to the Port of Miami today to wish a bon voyage to a special group of people sailing on a—" Mary Louise held up her fingers and indicated quotation marks, "'Santa Cruise.' Bianca, I hear you had some excitement out there today. . . ."

Bianca smiled brilliantly at the camera. "I sure did, Mary Louise. This was no *ordinary* bon voyage party . . ." She gave a quick background of the Santa Cruise and how it was a celebration of people who had done good deeds during the year. One group—the Oklahoma Readers and Writers—is celebrating what would have been the eightieth birthday of legendary mystery writer Left Hook Louie. Talking about mystery writers, there's a famous one on board: Nora Regan Reilly. A shot of the Reillys and the Meehans flashed onto the screen, as Bianca identified the celebrity passengers on the ship.

Then with great intensity, Bianca went into the story of the waiter, Ralph Knox, who had tried to escape from the police by jumping off the ship. "The passengers rushed to the rails and were taking bets on whether he could escape from the harbor police. Rest assured, he didn't.

"At first it was thought Knox was just being pursued for not making alimony payments—many of you ladies know what that's all about," she said, then nodded toward the anchor's desk. "Right, Mary Louise?" Without waiting for a reaction, she continued, "It turns out Ralph Knox is also a glib con artist who specializes in ingratiating himself to wealthy women on cruises. There are seven warrants out for his arrest. He is accused of persuading victims to invest hundreds of thousands of dollars in surefire investments that never materialized."

Bianca paused for breath. "As if that wasn't enough excitement for the embarking passengers, the sports director, attempting to demonstrate the rock-climbing wall, fell when a prong attached to the wall snapped under his foot and the handler let go of the rope attached to his harness."

Footage of Dudley landing with a thump appeared on the screen.

"Ouch," Bianca editorialized. She then briefly sketched in the background of the cruise ship's two previous owners. The ship had been built for Angus "Mac" MacDuffie, an eccentric oil baron from Palm Beach, who had promptly fallen on hard times. Even though he couldn't afford to maintain the ship, he refused to let it go. Instead, he hauled it into the vast backyard of his crumbling mansion, the bow facing the sea.

A photo of MacDuffie came up on the screen, his yachting cap pulled down over his forehead, his face half-covered with dark glasses, his tartan Bermuda shorts and sneakers his only apparel. "MacDuffie spent the last few years of his life sitting on the deck, scanning the horizon with his binoculars, and barking orders to a nonexistent crew," Bianca continued. "When he breathed his last, he was exactly where he wanted to be. On deck. His frequently uttered statement that he would 'never give up the ship' fueled rumors after his death that his ghost remained aboard.

"The next owner was a small corporation intending to use the yacht for entertaining clients. They did just enough restoration to make the ship seaworthy, took it out for a shakedown sail, and, alas, ran it aground. The corporation was disbanded soon after. The board of directors all blamed each other for purchasing it, but defended themselves, issuing a statement saying, 'MacDuffie put a hex on that ship. He doesn't want anyone else to enjoy it. We wouldn't be surprised if he's haunting it right now.' The next and present owner is Commodore Randolph Weed, who, ignoring the history of the ill-fated ship, has proclaimed it to be a 'once proud lady who only needed tender loving care.' "

As she wrapped up her piece, Bianca asked excitedly, "Is Commodore Weed right? Or is it possible that Angus 'Mac' MacDuffie is back on the high seas with the Santa Cruisers? If so, his favorite drink, the gin and tonic, will not be served to him by the waiter whose problems with the law sent him overboard, leaving a river of champagne and broken crystal in his wake. We'll keep you updated on the progress of this 'Do-Gooder' cruise. Maybe you're lucky you didn't do enough good this year to win a spot on this trip!" With an amused expression and a practiced wink, Bianca leaned forward slightly. "Don't forget. I always love hearing from you out there. My e-mail address is on the bottom of the screen."

"Thank you, Bianca," Mary Louise said condescendingly. "Now, Sam will tell us what's going on with that storm in the Caribbean. From what we can see, those Santa Cruisers must be experiencing at least the tip of it. . . ."

When Bianca returned to her desk, she checked her e-mail. She had distributed her card liberally at the Santa Cruise cocktail party with the hint that any gossipy items would be much appreciated. She clicked on an e-mail from a Loretta Marron, who was one of the Oklahoma Readers and Writers, and who had tried to tie up Bianca with a long story about being editor of her high school newspaper forty years ago.

> *Dear Bianca,*
>
> *News flash! One of the members of our group, Ivy Pickering, swears she saw the ghost of Left Hook Louie, the author we are honoring on this cruise. He was in the chapel jumping up and down as though he were getting ready for his next fight. I've enclosed his picture, which you can download. At first we thought she was joking. But now a lot of us are wondering—is the ghost of Left Hook Louie wandering around this ship? Already two of the Santa suits mysteriously disappeared from a locked supply room. Did Louie have anything to do with it?*
>
> *I'll keep in touch. Just call me Brenda Starr!!!!*
>
> > *Loretta*

Bianca was salivating. She had learned in Journalism 101 that everyone loved stories about the paranormal. And now she had one—and she'd already set the stage for it by talking about old MacDuffie. Quickly, she downloaded the picture of Left Hook Louie and gasped. He was a heavy-set man sitting at a typewriter, wearing only tartan shorts and boxing gloves. Bianca grabbed the picture of the heavy-set MacDuffie perched on the deck in his tartan shorts, holding his binoculars. He said he'd never give up the ship. Forget Left Hook Louie. Mac is the ghost on that ship!

She was already formulating her follow up story. *"Is there at least one extra passenger who doesn't belong on the Santa Cruise?"*

# 25

Dudley was barely inside his room when his beeper sounded. He did not need to look at it to know it was the Commodore. Glancing at his watch, Dudley saw that it was just eleven o'clock. When he was in port, Dudley loved to watch the local news. Tonight he was glad the news was not available on the ship. He didn't even want to *think* about what the reporter from the local station in Miami who'd attended the party this afternoon was saying about the Santa Cruise. He'd find out soon enough.

He picked up the phone from the night table and dialed the Commodore's suite. The Commodore grunted a hello.

In Dudley's best fake cheery voice, he chirped, "Commodore Weed, your favorite cruise director here. What can I do for you?"

"This is no time for levity," the Commodore grumbled. "Get up here immediately. I've been getting distress calls from land about the television coverage of this cruise and that loathsome waiter you hired!"

"I'll be right up," Dudley promised. "We'll get this all squared away, sir—"

The Commodore had already hung up.

Dudley hated his room but now looked longingly at the bed. To get undressed. Wash his hands and face. Brush his teeth. Floss. Get under the covers. It was not going to happen for a long time. If ever, he thought.

Winston answered the door of the Commodore's suite wearing a solemn expression, which immediately got under Dudley's skin. So Pluto isn't a planet anymore, Dudley thought sarcastically. Get over it. He sailed past Winston into the living room. The Commodore was in his admiral-of-the-fleet stance, shoulders rigid, hands clasped behind his back, staring out the window. When he turned around, Dudley was shocked to see that there were tears in his boss's eyes. The Commodore pointed in the direction of Miami. "They're snickering, Dudley. They're all making fun of us. I've received four calls in the last few minutes. You know what they're saying? 'You lose if you go on the Santa Cruise.' You lose! *I'm* losing. Lots of money. And now your big idea is a bust. That waiter is telling the cops that this ship is a joke." Commodore Weed's voice tightened. "They even showed a video of you falling on your bum at the rock-climbing wall. The newscaster had the nerve to call you the 'sports director.' "

Dudley was aghast. "They showed that video? Wasn't the coverage of the waiter swimming away enough?"

"Apparently not. We have entertained the city of Miami, and God knows where else the segment has been broadcast. Those kind of recorded moments are played and replayed on the Internet *millions* of times."

I'll never be able to go to my next high school reunion, Dudley thought. "But, sir . . ." he began. "Sometimes they say that any publicity is good publicity."

"Not in this case! Where's Eric?"

"I don't know."

"He's not answering his beeper. I want him here."

"Sir, I have a question."

"What?"

"They didn't mention Miss Pickering's hallucination, did they?"

The Commodore's misty eyes bulged. "No. But I'm sure that will be on the morning news. How many of our do-gooders are on cell phones at this very moment reporting on every last thing that has happened since we left Miami?"

"Sir, most cell phone coverage has faded by now. Only if you have a special world phone can you make and receive calls."

"Then they're calling from their rooms! I'm sure someone will get through! Summon Eric! We have to be ready with a dignified response to this disgraceful gossip."

# 26

"Do you hear what I hear?" Bull's-Eye asked Highbridge, who had curled himself into a fetal position.

"This is no time for Christmas carols," Highbridge snapped, as the rain relentlessly pelted every inch of their bodies.

"No, you idiot. I think Eric is singing a Christmas song. Listen."

"Who could hear anything with this wind?"

"Shut up. He must be looking for us."

The faint sound of Eric's voice was drifting toward them. Highbridge strained as he made out the words Eric was singing. It was a line from "Santa Claus Is Comin' to Town."

"He knows if you've been bad or good . . ."

"He's off-key," Highbridge muttered.

"At least he's trying to find us," Bull's-Eye snapped. "What do you want him to do, call out our names?"

The two men struggled to their feet and peered around the side of the barn. Eric was standing at the first hole, singing his heart out.

"Pssst. We're here," Bull's-Eye called to him.

Eric hurried over to them. "I've looked everywhere for you."

"Well, you found us," Bull's-Eye said. "Now what?"

"Some guy had an accident in the dining room and is in the infirmary. He'll be there at least overnight," Eric told them. "I have a pass key to his room. Follow me, but we have to be careful. They're cleaning up the buffet in the Lido and we can't let them see us. We'll have to crawl past the windows."

Three minutes later, as thoroughly drenched as if they'd been swimming in the ocean, the trio, traveling fifty feet apart, finally made it to Crater's room.

Highbridge ran into the bathroom and turned on the hot water in the shower. Bull's-Eye peeled off the wet Santa suit and stood in the tartan shorts that Ivy had described. He grabbed a bathrobe with the insignia of the Royal Mermaid from the closet and put it on. He then yanked a blanket from the bed and wrapped himself in it. "I'm going to get pneumonia. Is there a bar in here?"

Eric's beeper went off. He glanced at it. "It's my

143

uncle. He's been trying to reach me. There's a minibar in the cabinet. I'll be back."

After Eric left, Tony poured a miniature bottle of scotch into a glass and sat down on the bed. He had the feeling that Highbridge was going to use up all the hot water on the ship. As he took one strong gulp of the scotch, he looked around the room and noticed a remote control on the bed. He flicked on the television, not sure if he'd find anything other than a lecture about Fishbowl Island or a safety video explaining what to do if the ship was sinking. But when the screen lit up, Tony was shocked to see his mug shot staring back at him.

"Authorities are questioning Bingo Mullens about his association with Tony Pinto, who disappeared from his home on Christmas Day. Pinto is believed to be trying to flee the country, and an informer has told the FBI that Bingo Mullens was making inquiries to find someone willing to smuggle him out."

The scotch burned a hole in Pinto's gut. Bingo might give me up, he thought. He'll end up in Podunk in the Witness Protection Program, pretending to be a shoe salesman.

"Bingo, if you rat on me," Tony said aloud, "I'll kill you. The last guy who ratted on me has gotten away so far. But you won't. I swear to you, you won't."

# 27

When they got back to their stateroom, while getting ready for bed, Regan and Jack chatted about their first day at sea.

"I can't believe Alvirah talked us into this," Regan said, standing in the doorway of the bathroom as she was brushing her teeth. "I can just imagine what my father is saying to my mother."

"We both know that Alvirah is a magnet for trouble," Jack said as he kicked off his shoes. "But I will say that for a cruise that's supposed to be a tribute to the 'milk of human kindness,' there's a lot of strange stuff going on."

"I agree," Regan said. "If one of the crew members had problems with the law, that should have been discovered before he was hired. Who knows who else might be on board this ship? Whoever stole the Santa suits is obviously still with us, and if Ivy did really see someone, he obviously doesn't want to make himself known."

"Tomorrow morning, I'll see if I can get a passenger and crew list from Dudley. The office can do a quick check on everyone to see if any red flags come up." Jack flipped on the television. The news segments that were fed to the ship repeated over and over. A photo of Bull's-Eye Tony Pinto came up on the screen again. "Regan," Jack said. "Come here."

Regan stepped out of the bathroom. "What?"

They both listened as it was reported that Tony Pinto's fellow criminal, Bingo Mullens, was suspected of being the one who arranged his escape. "Look at his face, Regan," Jack said. "Bull's-Eye certainly does look a lot like that prizefighter author, doesn't he?"

"He sure does. And he's on the loose." Regan raised her eyebrows. "Maybe he's the one Ivy saw tonight."

They both laughed.

The ship gave a particularly strong lurch. "If he is on board, I hope he doesn't run into Alvirah," Jack commented. "Let's go to bed."

Regan smiled. "An offer I can't refuse."

# 28

Not dripping but still thoroughly wet, Eric let himself into the Commodore's suite, fully expecting a frosty reception. He had not responded to his beeper immediately, as his uncle always expected him to do. Worse, he had not responded to three separate summons, which he knew the Commodore would consider outright mutiny. He had his explanation ready.

The Commodore and Dudley were seated on the couch. They both gave him a dirty look when he entered the living room. Eric could tell that Dudley was thrilled he was in trouble.

"Uncle Randolph—" he began.

"You look like a drowned rat!" the Commodore barked. "You're hardly the spit-and-polish appearance I expect of every officer on the *Royal Mermaid.*" He paused. "As long as I can keep it afloat."

"Sir, I'm soaked because of my concern for our passengers. I heard people talking about how much fun it would be to sit outside in the storm. I scoured the decks to make sure no one was that crazy. I know how foolish people can be, not realizing how dangerous that is."

"Did you find anybody?" Dudley asked in a montone, his eyebrows raised.

"Thank God, no," Eric answered vehemently. "I feel so much better knowing everyone is safe on board. The passageways are empty. Everyone is tucked in for the night, hopefully being rocked to sleep in the comfort of the *Royal Mermaid,* a protective cradle in this stormy sea."

The Commodore raised his hand. "I didn't realize you were that poetic, Eric. Get out of those wet clothes and get back in here. On the double. We have a crisis on our hands."

"Everyone was warned that it was not safe to go out on deck in the storm. That should have been enough," Dudley said primly.

In his room, Eric quickly peeled off his clothes and put on a jogging suit. When he returned to the Commodore's living room, his uncle was staring at the locked glass cabinet on the wall opposite the couch.

"Eric," the Commodore said, pointing to the cabinet, "I didn't tell you because I wanted it to be a wonderful surprise. We have an extra passenger on this voyage."

Eric's knees turned to water. "An extra passenger? Who?"

"Grandma."

"Grandma? Grandma died eight years ago."

"Your grandmother's ashes," Dudley injected. "They're in the silver box in the glass case."

"Grandma was cremated?" Eric asked, stunned.

"It was her wish to be cremated. In her last hours she told me she knew I would realize my dream to own a cruise ship, and when that happened she wanted me to take her on the first sailing and scatter her ashes at sea."

"Nobody tells me anything," Eric complained.

"If you had attended her funeral you would have known," the Commodore admonished. "My three ex-wives attended. They had great respect for your grandma. Your ex-aunt Beatrice, your ex-aunt Johanna, and your ex-aunt Reeney all sat together, crying their eyes out. When I spoke to Reeney not too long ago, I told her the time had finally come and I was planning to scatter Grandma's ashes on this maiden cruise. She wanted to join us, but even I have a limit to my patience. Now this cruise has been marred by bad publicity—"

"How do you know?" Eric asked, his heart skipping a beat. "What are people saying about this cruise?"

The Commodore gave him the rundown. "It's such disrespect to your grandmother's memory. She did so much good in her life that I thought it would honor her memory to have her final send-off not only from my first cruise but surrounded by good, good, good people. Now, it's all become a mockery—" The Commodore's voice cracked, and he reached in his pocket for his handkerchief. "It's so unfair," he said, wiping his eyes. "Not a single person is paying to be on this cruise. Not a single one! And everybody's making fun of me!"

Eric sat down next to his uncle, awkwardly put his arm around him, and was shocked when the Commodore buried his head in his shoulder. "There, there, Uncle Randolph."

"Grandma doesn't deserve this. At dinner tomorrow, I was going to make an announcement that my dear mother's ashes would be lowered to the sea early Wednesday morning on what would have been her ninety-fifth birthday. When Dudley suggested we have this Santa Cruise that is costing me a fortune, the fact that your grandmother's birthday would fall during the cruise made me realize it was meant to be. I was going to tell our passengers tomorrow night that there would be a brief but moving ceremony in the chapel at dawn, and I would be so touched if anyone joined me. I know, of course, Eric, that you will be at her final send-off. I think you've matured in these last eight years. But now, I just don't know what to do—"

Eric looked over at the glass case. "Hello, Grandma," he said softly.

Tears flowed from the Commodore's eyes. "That beautiful woman is in that exquisite silver box. Under lock and key."

"You were always so protective of her."

The Commodore nodded. "In life and in death. I've heard terrible stories about ashes of the beloved being spilled by careless or clueless parlor maids. That's why I've guarded those ashes with my life."

"Where did you keep Grandma all these years?"

"Her urn was in a cabinet exactly like this one in my bedroom at home. It is fireproof, waterproof, and theft proof. I haven't discussed it much. . . . It was too painful. But from me, Grandma gets only loving care."

Dudley cleared his throat. "Sir, I have been through many crises before and it's how the situation is handled that is important. For goodness' sake, I was on a cruise ship that accidentally sailed without any desserts or dessert makings on board. The pastry chef had quit and turned out to be quite spiteful. He canceled the orders for all the flour, chocolate, etc., etc. His last-minute substitute didn't have the ingredients to whip up so much as a Twinkie. There was a revolt among the passengers, but we turned it into an advantage. We had round-the-clock exercise classes and gave a free cruise to the person who lost the most weight. Someone won by a tenth of a pound."

Dudley stood and began to pace the room. "I suggest we send out a press release tonight stressing the purity of this cruise, the sweet story of your mother, and the charitable achievements of everyone on board. And if the media can't understand that, well then they should be ashamed of themselves! You should go ahead with your plans to have the beautiful ceremony for Mother Weed. Tomorrow, another press release will go out hailing the new day and how lucky these freeloaders—I mean guests—are to have spent their first night on the high seas on this beautiful ship."

The Commodore wiped his eyes and blew his nose. "I'm so blessed to have the two of you. Believe it or not, I miss being married. Your companionship means the world to me."

Dudley stood. "I will go back to my cabin and work on the first press release."

"Sir, you should go in and get some sleep," Eric said to his uncle.

"Eventually. But now I'm going to stretch out on the couch and visit with Grandma. I don't have much time left with her before she belongs to the sea. . . ."

Inwardly, Eric panicked. He had to go back downstairs to check on Bull's-Eye and High-bridge. How could he get away?

"Eric, I insist you go in and take a hot shower and get to bed. I can't have you getting sick. If we're going to pull ourselves up by the bootstraps and make this cruise a success, we all have to be in top form. Now, say good-night to Grandma. . . ."

# 29

The scotch did not calm Bull's-Eye down. It increased his sense of frustration. He felt trapped. If Bingo gave him up, it wouldn't take long for the Feds to arrive in a helicopter, or pull up on a boat, and that would be the end.

He got up from the bed, poured himself another scotch, pulled open the drawer next to the liquor cabinet, and found a jar of peanuts, a package of Hershey's Kisses, and a roll of breath mints. It took about a minute and a half to polish them off. If Highbridge was going to use up all the hot water, he was going to eat everything he could get his hands on.

Most of the other drawers were empty. Whoever was staying in this room had packed lightly for the cruise. Then, in the last drawer he opened, Bull's-Eye found a tube of gray paste. He read the label. It was costume makeup. A spark of suspicion, the kind of instinct that had always served him well, made Tony curious to check out everything else in the room.

He walked over to the closet, opened the door, and the light went on automatically. Three jackets and a tuxedo were hanging there. Forty-four Extra Large, he noted. I could wear these, he thought. He checked the pockets, and in the third one his fingers closed around a gun. It was a Glock, a weapon he preferred. Who is this guy, he wondered as he transferred the gun to the pocket of his robe. Then he reached up and felt along the ledge under the life jackets. His fingers touched soft leather. Some kind of bag, he guessed, as he pulled it down carefully. It was an expensive-looking briefcase that zipped on three sides and had no handle.

He brought it back to the bed, picked up the scotch, took another gulp, and opened the brief-case. Grunting in surprise, he stared down at what appeared to be a dozen packets of one-hundred-dollar bills. Bull's-Eye dumped the contents onto the bed. Three United States passports tumbled from a pocket. He opened one of them, and when he saw the picture, his body stiffened. Quickly, he looked at the second and third pictures. The three faces looked entirely different, but close study showed they were the same man. And it was a man he knew.

Eddie Gordon, the rat whose testimony had sent Tony's father to prison. Bull's-Eye had been looking for him for fifteen years. Gordon went under different aliases. From the date of issue on the passports, the latest was Harry Crater.

He's not on this cruise because he's a do-gooder, Bull's-Eye thought. I wonder what he's up to. Eric said he's in the infirmary. Another thought struck him—could Eddie Gordon be faking his need to be there?

Doesn't matter, he told himself. Whether he's faking or not, by the time I get through with him, he'll be beyond medical care.

# 30

Ted Cannon had always been a light sleeper. He became one even more so during the months when Joan was sick, and he was tuned to the slightest change in her breathing. He had been glad to get one of the few single cabins on the ship. It was half the size of the others, but perfectly comfortable and had a private balcony. The one disadvantage was that it had a connecting door to the next room—good for a family traveling with children, but not so great for two different parties who didn't want to hear each other's television playing.

Ted knew that his neighbor, the sickly looking guy, Crater, had been taken to the infirmary when he fell at dinner. As Ted was getting ready for bed, he heard the murmur of Crater's television. I'm glad, he thought. He can't have been too badly hurt. On the other hand, my best hope of a decent night's sleep is to doze off before I do too much thinking. And if the television is on for too long, I'm out of luck.

The ship was still rocking, and it felt good to get into bed and pull up the blanket. Last night at this time, I was telling myself I made a mistake signing up for this cruise, he thought. But actually it's been kind of fun. Alone in the dark, he smiled as the events of the day ran through his mind. At dinner, he hadn't minded being asked to visit from table to table between courses. He enjoyed talking to his fellow passengers. The people on this cruise really are nice and genuine, he reflected, like the Ryans, who are on board because they'd raised money for research into a rare disease that had taken their son's life. The way they had directed their grief toward something positive and helpful to so many others made Ted wonder if there was something to his son's gentle hint, in so many words, that he was letting himself wallow in self-pity. Not the way Bill put it of course, but it was the gist of what he was saying. In fact, Ted thought uncomfortably, that's exactly the way Joan would have put it. She'd have no use for me continuing to feel sorry for myself.

In the next room, the television had been turned off, but he could hear drawers opening and closing, then the sound of voices. Maybe someone's in there helping Crater get settled for the night, Ted reasoned as he turned on one side and pulled the blanket even closer up around his face to cover his ears.

As he started to fall asleep, he thought how glad he was that he had stopped to ask Maggie Quirk about Ivy Pickering. Maggie was funny in a self-deprecating way. She didn't wear a ring, so she probably wasn't married. She had told him she was planning to jog at six A.M. If the storm calmed down, he'd get up and put on his jogging suit, too.

Ted was an early riser, but to be sure he didn't oversleep, he turned on the light and set the alarm for five thirty.

# 31

Like most of the passengers, Maggie and Ivy went directly to bed when they reached their room. Standing up wasn't easy in the storm, and anyhow it had been a long day. Maggie fell asleep promptly, but at about quarter of four woke to find Ivy sitting on the edge of her bed. Maggie turned on the light.

"Are you all right, Ivy?" she asked. "You haven't seen another ghost, have you?"

"Very funny, Maggie," Ivy said, laughing in spite of herself. "I'd rather be up because I saw a ghost than feel the way I do. I'm so queasy. And I'm shivering."

"Let's go down to the infirmary right away," Maggie suggested as she started to get out of bed.

"Oh, I couldn't make it all the way down there. I feel too dizzy. I'll just lie down and see if it will pass."

Maggie reached for her robe. "Then I'll go and

see if I can get you an ear patch and whatever else they're giving out."

"I don't want you to walk around the ship alone at this hour," Ivy said, then moaned. "But if you insist," she finished feebly. "I never thought I was the type to get seasick. . . ."

"I'll get a wet washcloth for your forehead and then run downstairs."

# 32

By the time Highbridge got out of the shower, Bull's-Eye had replaced the contents of the briefcase, zipped it up tight, and hidden the case under the bed. He knew what he was going to do, and one of the early lessons he'd learned in his life of crime was, "Loose lips sink ships."

The sight of the candy wrappers and empty jar of nuts infuriated Highbridge. "You couldn't have saved me a crumb?"

"I was hungry," Bull's-Eye replied, his tone ugly. "I still am."

The two men had been reduced to sullen silence. When Bull's-Eye went into the bathroom, he saw that Highbridge had hung up his Santa suit and stuffed towels in the arms and legs to prevent wrinkles. When Tony asked Highbridge why he was being such a fussbudget, the Bean Counter said he planned to go to the early risers' buffet and grab some food. "But none for you," he'd added.

By the time Bull's-Eye got out of the shower, Highbridge was already asleep on his side of the queen-sized bed. Bull's-Eye lay down and turned out the light. How could Highbridge sleep at a time like this? he wondered. Bull's-Eye's mind was racing—he had to get his cards. And this was his only chance to find Eddie Gordon. Once he was off this ship and on his way to Fishbowl Island, he'd probably never run into him again. He owed it to his father to whack Gordon. If he didn't at least try, he'd have to live in shame for the rest of his life.

He knew it was risky. But he had to make the attempt.

Bull's-Eye planned to wait until four A.M., when the odds were that the ship's passageways would be deserted. He had heard somewhere that more people die around four A.M. than at any other time in the twenty-four-hour cycle. As Bull's-Eye closed his eyes, knowing he wouldn't sleep, he hoped that he'd successfully add someone new to that statistic.

At three thirty, unable to wait any longer, Bull's-Eye got out of bed. He tighened the belt of the terry cloth robe, tossed a thick towel around his neck, and put on a pair of Gordon's dark sunglasses that he found on the bedside table. He was grateful they weren't prescription.

The dimly lit corridor was deserted. At the elevator bank he discovered a diagram of the ship, listing where all the different rooms were located. As he expected, the infirmary was on the lowest level. From the diagram, he could tell which companionway to take. He made his way there without encountering a single soul.

With infinite care, he opened the door of the infirmary and found himself in an eerily quiet and empty waiting room. A prominent sign on the desk read NURSE ON DUTY. PRESS BUZZER FOR ASSISTANCE.

He walked behind the desk and in a stealthy movement opened the door to the inner sanctum. Moving slowly, guided by the soft baseboard lighting, he peered into a small office on his left where he noticed the silhouette of a nurse asleep in a reclining chair. Her heavy, deep breathing reassured him that she would not be a problem, at least for the moment. For her own sake, he hoped she would continue to sleep.

In the second room on the right, he spotted the man who had caused his family so much misery. Even in the semidarkness, he recognized the profile of Eddie Gordon, the man known as

Crater. Bull's-Eye thought of his poor mother making the long trek to the federal prison in Allentown, Pennsylvania, once a month for fifteen years to see his father. All those years looking at his father's empty place at the dinner table. "This is for you, Papa," he whispered as he stepped into the darkened room, eased a pillow from behind Crater's head, and with a swift, decisive movement, held it over the sleeping man's face.

From somewhere inside his drug-induced sleep, Crater/Gordon was having a nightmare. He couldn't breathe. He was choking. He began to gurgle and flail the air with his hands. It was real. It wasn't a nightmare. The instinct to survive made him slip his hands under the pillow that was covering his face and yank on it fiercely. He felt strong thumbs pressing against his neck. A voice was whispering, "This is what you deserve."

"Aahhhhhhhhhh." Crater knew his scream was coming out as a whisper.

The sound of the buzzer from the waiting room echoed from the nurse's office down the hallway.

Bull's-Eye froze. Wrestling to keep the pillow pressed on Crater's face, he realized that the buzzer would surely wake up the nurse, and that whoever had pushed it was in the waiting room.

He did the only thing he could do—he tossed

the pillow aside, rushed out, and hid in the room next door.

"Aaahhhh," Crater began yelling.

Bull's-Eye watched as the nurse ran down the hallway and headed into Crater's room. The towel high around his neck, the dark glasses on, he opened the door to the outer waiting room. His hand half covering his face, he left the infirmary without glancing at the woman who had just turned to take a seat.

Crater was struggling to figure out what had happened. He hadn't imagined it, someone *had* tried to kill him. He had always had the suspicion that the big boss had placed another person on the inside on this job. Maybe whoever it is had been afraid he'd talk under sedation and had tried to kill him. He had to get to his room and keep the door double-locked until the helicopter arrived.

"What happened, Mr. Crater?" the nurse asked as she flipped on the light.

"I had a bad dream," he croaked.

"But your neck is all red. And why is your pillow at the foot of the bed?"

"I'm a rough sleeper."

"Dr. Gephardt said you could have another sedative if necessary."

"No!" He knew that until he got off this ship,

he wasn't safe closing an eye. Oddly enough, his back felt better after the struggle. "I'm going back to my room."

"Absolutely not. Doctor's orders. You'll have to speak to him when he comes on duty at seven o'clock."

"I'm out of here at 7:01."

But the nurse had already left the room.

A few minutes later, an exhausted Maggie was slowly making her way back to her room with an ear patch for Ivy. When she finally settled into her bed, she felt bleary-eyed and uneasy but had no intention of changing her plans to jog at six A.M.

Unless her antenna was way off, Ted Cannon would be up on the track right around that time.

# 33

Alvirah woke up at quarter of six. Willy was still asleep, seemingly in the same position he'd been in all night. The movement of the ship had subsided to a gentle roll. Alvirah got out of bed quietly. In the bathroom, she splashed cold water on her face and brushed her teeth. She slipped on a jogging suit and snapped on her sunburst pin. I do my best thinking in the morning with a cup of coffee, she thought. And I know they serve coffee, juice, and bagels from six to seven in the Lido before they open for the full breakfast.

She scrawled a note for Willy, propped it against the lamp on the desk, then with infinite care opened the door quietly and stepped out into the passageway. Closing it with the faintest of clicks, she hurried down the corridor and was startled when the door to the Commodore's suite opened. A sleepy-looking Eric, dressed in a rumpled jogging suit, appeared.

"The early bird gets the worm," Alvirah said cheerfully, then tried to seize the opportunity to corner Eric for a chat. "Join me for coffee. You were so nice, giving up your room to us. I expect to do a very favorable column for my newspaper about the cruise, and I'd love to feature you in it."

Eric did not miss the sharp glint in Alvirah's eyes and was aware that she was studying him carefully. He had pretended to go to bed in his room, but left the door open enough so he could see when his uncle either went to bed or fell asleep on the couch. The trouble was that Eric had fallen asleep before his uncle and had only just awakened with the shocking realization that it was early morning and Crater could return to his cabin at any time. Eric called down to the infirmary and was told by the nurse that Crater's back was definitely much better and that he insisted on being discharged as soon as the doctor came on duty at seven A.M. That meant Eric had only one hour to get Bull's-Eye and Highbridge out of Crater's room and hide them until Winston had straightened up the suite and he could sneak them into his own room.

"Thank you, Mrs. Meehan," he told Alvirah, "but I have to go down to the infirmary and check on Mr. Crater, then get back up and dress for the day." He laughed and patted Alvirah's arm. "My uncle might seem easygoing, but he runs a tight ship, as they say."

A tight ship? Alvirah thought. Judging from what I've seen, this ship is going to hell in a handbasket. "Another time," she suggested sweetly. "Don't you just love dawn's early light? I swear my brain tingles when I get up with the birds. I guess you know I have the reputation of being a good amateur sleuth. When I'm trying to figure out what's going on, I put my thinking cap on and, lo and behold, I often come up with an answer."

For the briefest of moments, the muscles in Eric's neck tightened. "What are you trying to figure out now?" he asked, trying to sound as though he was amused.

"Oh, this and that," Alvirah answered airily. She was dying to ask Eric if he liked potato chips, but knew the question would come out of left field and would not be well received. "For example, I'd love to figure out who took those Santa suits. They might not be worth much, but no matter how you slice it, it's still theft."

Eric didn't want to continue the conversation. With every word the woman uttered, he felt his heart pounding harder in his chest. This tiresome old bag was playing with him, he knew it. "I'm sure you're quite the sleuth, Mrs. Meehan," he said. "Enjoy your coffee while I check on our patient."

By now they had reached the elevators, but Eric darted down the nearby steps. He must like to get exercise, walking all the way down to the infirmary, Alvirah thought. I'll spare my knees. She pushed the DOWN button and waited.

At 6:04, she was in the Lido at the coffeemaker, pouring that first wonderful cup for herself. Behind the heavy swinging doors, she could hear the kitchen workers clattering dishes. I guess I'm the first customer, she thought. But glancing out the window she saw a tall Santa with a tray of coffee, juice, and bagels, walking rapidly along the deck, away from the Lido, toward the stern.

She wondered if it could be that nice Mr. Cannon. He was one of the taller Santas. She hurried over and pushed open the glass door. "Hey Santa!" she boomed, a smile in her voice. The Santa glanced over his shoulder but instead of slowing up, increased his pace. It was then that Alvirah saw, or thought she saw, that he had only one bell on his cap. She started to run after him, but the deck was slippery and the next thing she knew the coffee had gone flying and she had gone down like a ton of bricks, smashing her head into the side of one of the deck chairs.

For a moment, she was totally stunned and gasping for breath. Her head began to explode with pain, and she felt blood gushing down her face. Dazed, she looked up. The Santa was nowhere to be seen. I'm going to pass out, she thought, but first, with her left hand, in a reflex action, she snapped on the microphone of her sunburst pin. "I'm sure he saw me," she began, her voice groggy. "He was tall. I thought it was Ted Cannon. I think he had only one bell on his cap. My forehead is bleeding. I fell chasing him and now I'm sprawled on the deck—"

Then Alvirah fainted. After that, she had a blurry memory of people around her, of being lifted onto a stretcher, of something cold being pressed to her forehead, of riding in an elevator. When she regained consciousness, she opened her eyes to find Willy peering anxiously down at her. "That was some fall, honey," he said. "Don't try to move."

Her head was aching fiercely but other than that, Alvirah hoped she hadn't done herself any damage. She squeezed her toes and fingers. They felt okay. She shifted her shoulders and was relieved that her back still moved.

Dr. Gephardt, his white uniform jacket not yet fully buttoned, was standing beside Willy. "Mrs. Meehan," he said, "that was a nasty blow to your head. I'll stitch up your forehead, and then we'll take an X-ray. I want you to take it easy for the next several hours."

"I'll be fine," Alvirah protested. "But believe me, there's something very funny going on on this ship."

"What do you mean, honey?" Willy asked.

Alvirah's head was one solid ache, but her brain was beginning to clear. "I saw one of those Santa Clauses right after I got coffee. I thought it was that nice Ted Cannon—"

"He's in the waiting room," Willy interrupted. "He was jogging with Maggie and they came around the corner and found you lying on the deck. You were talking—"

"Into my microphone," Alvirah said.

"Well, then you passed out."

"I know Ted wouldn't have ignored me. But the Santa I saw *did*. I yelled to him. He turned and looked at me and then kept going. And he had only one bell on his cap! I'm telling you . . . he must have been wearing one of the stolen suits. We've got to find out who that Santa is and where he is! Let's get Dudley and Regan and Jack."

"Regan, Jack, Luke, and Nora are right here in the waiting room."

"Send them in!" Alvirah ordered.

"Mrs. Meehan, I think you need to stay calm—" Gephardt began.

"I'm okay," Alvirah insisted. "I've taken harder knocks than this. My family is famous for thick skulls. I'll never stay calm knowing there's a thief who may be up to no good on this ship!"

From the next room they heard a raised voice. "I hear the doctor. I want him in here *now!*"

"If you'll excuse me," Gephardt said hurriedly as he dashed out.

"That must be Crater," Alvirah told Willy. "He's got a pretty powerful set of vocal chords for someone who looked like he was about to keel over yesterday."

"He sounds better now," Willy agreed. "Let me get the Reillys."

"Tell Maggie and Ted to come in, too. We've got work to do."

In the couple of minutes it took everyone to get to her room, Alvirah's thoughts turned to Eric. He was supposed to have come directly down to check on Mr. Crater. Her hunch was that he hadn't made it.

"Alvirah! Are you all right?" Nora asked as they all crowded into the room.

"I'm fine. Never better."

"What happened?"

Alvirah recounted the story of the unfriendly Santa. Ted and Maggie had already explained to the Reillys how they had found Alvirah lying on the deck. "I'm almost certain he was wearing a cap with only one bell," Alvirah told them. "We've got to have Dudley round up all eight Santa suits and make sure they all have two bells on the caps. If they do, then whoever I saw was wearing one of the stolen suits. What I've been thinking is we can enlist the other Santas to help us. We'll have to mark the Santa suits in some way so that we'll be able to pick out either of the stolen suits if someone wears them around the ship. . . . I think that someone must have stolen those suits so one or two people can get around this ship in disguise. I almost caught one of them."

"Are you *sure* he heard you call him?" Regan asked.

"Positive. He turned around. I couldn't see his face with that beard." She turned to Ted. "From the back I thought it might have been you. He was on the tall side."

Ted smiled. "I'm glad I have a reliable witness."

"That's me, Old Reliable," Maggie quipped.

Jack shook his head. "It makes sense that whoever stole the suits wanted to be able to get around the ship incognito. I don't think any of the real Santas would be expected to roll out of bed and put on their suit to go down and get coffee."

"It's ridiculous!" Alvirah cried. "There wasn't even anyone else down there for him to 'Ho-Ho-Ho' with. And he certainly didn't want to 'Ho-Ho-Ho' with *me*."

Willy grabbed her hand. "I always want to 'Ho-Ho-Ho' with you," he said.

"I know you do, Willy," Alvirah said fondly.

The nurse poked her head in the door. "How are we doing, Mrs. Meehan?"

"I'm doing fine," Alvirah answered pointedly. "What's *your* story?"

Regan knew that if there was one thing that got under Alvirah's skin, it was the collective "we" in a medical situation.

The nurse ignored her question. Glancing around the room, she noticed Maggie. "You're up early after having been here in the middle of the night. How's your friend?" she asked.

"She was still sleeping when I left." As the others looked at her inquiringly, Maggie explained. "The patch helped Ivy a lot."

"It was so stormy last night. My guess is you handed out a lot of those patches," Luke surmised.

"We were very busy until about midnight. Ms. Quirk was our only visitor after that, until Mrs. Meehan arrived."

Alvirah saw the look of disbelief on Maggie's face. "What is it, Maggie?" she asked.

"Nothing. It's just that I figured the man I saw coming out of this area through the waiting room last night was a patient."

The nurse started to speak, then hesitated. Dr. Gephardt was behind her and had clearly heard the exchange.

"Was there someone else in this area last night around the time Mr. Crater was having his nightmare?" Gephardt asked the nurse, his voice serious and deeply concerned.

"Certainly not that I'm aware of," the nurse answered crisply.

Dr. Gephardt turned to Maggie. "According to our records, you were here at four A.M."

"Yes, I was," Maggie said.

"And you say you saw a man coming out from this area into the waiting room?"

"Yes, I did. I was turned away from him, about to sit down, and he walked right past me."

"What did he look like?" Alvirah asked.

Maggie hesitated. "I knew something was bothering me, and I know this is going to sound crazy—"

"Say it anyway," Alvirah insisted.

Maggie shook her head and grimaced. "He looked like Left Hook Louie."

# 34

When Eric reached the deck where Crater's cabin was located, he looked down the corridor and saw Jonathan, the steward for that section, coming out of the end suite. Probably some of the awake-at-dawns sent for coffee, he thought, ducking back before he was spotted. He had absolutely no reason to be here, and if Jonathan caught a glimpse of him, he'd have to come up with some sort of explanation. Rather than stand at the elevator bank, he walked down the companionway for three decks, then turned and walked slowly back up again.

This time there was no sign of the steward. But, to his horror, he saw a tall Santa Claus he realized was Highbridge, carrying a tray tap on the door of Crater's room. An instant later, it was opened and just as quickly closed as Highbridge disappeared inside. Pass key in hand, Eric rushed down the long corridor and opened the door. Highbridge was setting the tray on the desk. Ripping off his beard, he looked at Eric.

"What a pleasant surprise! I thought you had crossed us off your list."

"I've got to get you out of here right away. Crater is demanding to come back to his cabin immediately. The doctor doesn't start work till seven, but Crater might just sign himself out."

Bull's-Eye was already wolfing down a bagel. With his mouth full, he snapped at Eric, "All right, Uncle's Boy, where do you propose to put us now?" Without waiting for an answer, he continued, "We'll be close enough to Fishbowl Island in twenty-three hours for our people to get us. We'd better make it." He gave Eric a cold stare.

By now Eric was terrified of Bull's-Eye. Being around him was like being in a cage with an angry lion. Eric tried to go back to the moments when he had made the deals to smuggle the two felons onto the ship. It had seemed so easy at the time. A million dollars each to conceal them for less than forty-eight hours. That broke down to more than forty-one thousand dollars an hour. How could he have refused a windfall like that? But now, if they were caught, both men would tell the cops he was their accomplice. Denying it would be useless. Eric knew that he could never pass a lie detector test.

He stared back at Bull's-Eye. "All this trouble started because you were jumping up and down in the chapel," he said defensively. "You were supposed to be wearing your Santa outfit so that if anyone had seen you, they would have thought you were praying or meditating or something. Now let's get out of here. Once I sneak you upstairs, I have to come back and clean up this place. Get dressed, Bull's-Eye."

"Don't blame this on *me,*" Bull's-Eye retorted. "Where are we going?"

"Back to the chapel."

"What are you, nuts?"

"It's temporary, until I can get you back in my room. There's no other place to hide you."

"You better hope your uncle doesn't end up praying for you in that chapel," Bull's-Eye said as he took a last swig of coffee. He had dropped his Santa outfit on the floor when he shed it and changed into the robe. Now a stream of muttered invectives rushed from his lips as he pulled on the wet, wrinkled pants and jacket. The beard was a soggy mass of sour-smelling fuzz. As he hooked it over his ears, he began to sneeze.

"I'll go first," Eric instructed. "Once we make it to the companionway we won't be likely to run into anyone. It's still too early." He opened the door a slit and listened. There was no sound in the corridor. Jonathan was nowhere in sight. "Come on," he whispered sharply to Bull's-Eye and Highbridge.

It was only six twenty-five. The ship was very quiet. On the Boat Deck, Winston wouldn't show up for at least another twenty minutes. He's been told to bring in the Commodore's breakfast at seven fifteen every morning. But Uncle Randolph will be awake soon, Eric realized. He does yoga from six forty-five to seven fifteen, and he told me he's going to start giving himself extra time so he can perfect the lotus position.

One deck up and safe so far. Two. Three. The sound of silence calmed Eric's quivering nerves. They turned right and down the corridor to the chapel. Eric opened the door and looked in. No early worshipers, thank God. He led the two crooks up the aisle. "Get under the altar and *don't move* this time," he ordered. "I'll be back for you in a couple of hours. Once my uncle's butler makes the bed and cleans up, he won't go near my room until tonight. I'll have food there for you."

As Bull's-Eye squatted down, Eric noticed for the first time that he had a zippered leather briefcase under his arm. "Where did you get that?" he demanded.

"I found it outside while we were getting

soaked last night," Bull's-Eye said sarcastically. "Something else. I left my cards in the night table drawer in your first room, where we're supposed to be right now. Get them. They're very important."

Cards! Eric thought of Willy Meehan offering him the deck of cards. "I didn't know—" he began.

"What do you mean you didn't know?"

"Nothing. Nothing. I'll get them. I've got to go *now.*"

It was 6:31. Eric rushed out of the chapel and a minute later was inside the supply room, near his uncle's suite. He grabbed towels and wash cloths and two folded robes to replace the ones Highbridge and Bull's-Eye had used, dumping them in a plastic bag. Those two could have been a little neater, he thought, remembering the candy wrappers he'd seen on the desk. Why didn't they put a sign on the door? CROOKS IN RESIDENCE. DO DROP IN.

Never one to clean up after himself, he worked with enviable speed when he got back to Crater's room. He replaced the wet towels with fresh ones, rinsed and dried the drinking glasses, polished the mirror over the cabinet and the glass door of the shower, and hung the fresh robes in the closet. During dinner last night, Jonathan had already turned down Crater's bed and drawn the curtains. Eric fluffed the bed pillows and smoothed the spread. At least whatever sleeping those two jerks had done had been on top of the spread so the sheets and blanket were neat. Had Bull's-Eye taken that valise from this room? Eric wondered nervously. If so, there'd be hell to pay.

It was ten of seven. He had to get down to the infirmary and be able to report to his uncle that he'd seen Crater there. First he ran up to the pool area and dropped the soiled towels and robes on a beach chair. He reached the infirmary just as Crater was being wheeled into the waiting room area. Dr. Gephardt was beside him, saying, "Mr. Crater, your records indicate you have a serious health problem. When you get to your room, I suggest you go to bed and stay there. You've had a shock to your nervous system."

Crater's face was flushed. Eric could see two purple bruises on either side of his neck. Did the medical attendants cause that when they moved him? he wondered.

"Mr. Crater," he began. "My uncle, the Commodore—"

Crater looked at him suspiciously. "Go away," he snarled.

"We're all so sorry this happened. I will escort you to your room," Eric said firmly.

"Eric, may I see you for a moment?" Gephardt asked.

"Not now. I want to get Mr. Crater to his room where he can be comfortable."

"Then please come back."

Uh-oh, Eric thought as he began to push the wheelchair. "Right away," he promised.

Outside Crater's room, Eric asked him for his key. No use letting Crater know I can get in on my own, he decided. He was relieved to see that looking through Crater's eyes the cabin appeared exactly as it would have, if he had returned last night. Crater stood up. "All right, you've seen me here. Now leave me alone."

This guy is scared, Eric thought. Maybe I'm crazy but he looks as though he's even afraid of me. "I'm on my way, sir. Let me know if you need anything."

"I do. Find my cell phone. I already told them in the infirmary to look for it. It must have fallen out of my pocket when those brats floored me."

"I'll find it, don't you worry. Feel better, sir." At least I have something to report to Uncle Randolph, he thought, cheering himself up as he pushed the wheelchair back to the infirmary.

Dr. Gephardt was in his office. "Come in, Eric," he said quietly.

184

Eric stayed in the doorway. "Make it quick. I have to get showered and dressed. My uncle will be wondering what happened to me."

"Eric, you must have noticed those bruises on Mr. Crater's neck?"

"I did."

"Someone tried to kill him last night."

"What are you talking about?" Eric asked, his voice incredulous.

"I'm talking about the attempted murder of one of my patients. We've got to let the Commodore know and sound some kind of alarm."

Eric's brain began to focus. "Did Crater *say* someone tried to kill him?"

"He denies it."

"Then what are we talking about?"

Gephardt related the story and the fact that a four A.M. visitor to the infirmary, a Maggie Quirk, had seen an unknown person leaving through the waiting room.

"You're crazy," Eric said. "Why would Crater deny it if someone tried to suffocate him?"

"That's a good question. But it happened. If Ms. Quirk hadn't happened to have come along and rung that buzzer, Nurse Rich would have found a suffocated corpse when she finally woke up."

Eric seized on the fact that Crater had denied

the attempt. "Do you realize how ridiculous it would be to claim there was an attempted murder if the victim denies it happened?"

"No less, perhaps, than letting a would-be killer wander around this ship! There should be a general search for him immediately. As a matter of fact, Ms. Quirk reported that the intruder bears a resemblance to Left Hook Louie, the writer whose photos are all over the ship. That is the same description Ms. Pickering gave of the man she saw in the chapel last night, isn't it?"

Eric froze. He had to be talking about Bull's-Eye. Had that idiot left the room last night? He started to sputter, "Th . . . , Th . . . , Then you suggest we start a search for a *ghost?* Do you realize an action like that would finish this cruise line? Have a little loyalty, Doctor, and forget these histrionics."

Alvirah had gotten up to go to the bathroom and caught every word of the exchange. Oh boy, oh boy, she thought, this is really something. It's a good thing I bumped my head and got in on all this.

# 35

After her startling announcement in Alvirah's room, Maggie had been almost apologetic. "I know I sound crazy," she had said, referring to her impression of the nocturnal visitor coming through the waiting room.

"The sad thing is, given what's gone on around this place, you don't sound crazy at all," Alvirah had declared.

As Maggie and Ted were leaving to resume their interrupted jog, Dr. Gephardt had nervously asked the Reillys to leave. He wanted to stitch up the cut on Alvirah's forehead and take an X-ray. "It won't take long," he promised. "And then, if Mrs. Meehan feels well enough, she can go and relax on one of our deck chairs. But no running any races," he tried to joke.

The Reillys, Regan and Jack, Nora and Luke, made their way up to the Lido. It was now beautiful outside, but after they selected food from the buffet, they carried their trays to a corner table inside the restaurant. It was a good place both to observe and to talk. Regan had put a call into Dudley, filled him in on Alvirah's accident, and asked him to join them.

"It's urgent," she told him.

Dudley, who had been toiling half the night on his second press release extolling the happy atmosphere on the Santa Cruise, almost fainted when he heard about the nasty Santa. It has to be someone wearing one of the stolen suits, he thought. Even that miserable Bobby Grimes wouldn't have left Mrs. Meehan sprawled on the deck. "I'll be right there," he croaked. Papers were scattered on his bed, his desk, and on the floor, the result of his efforts at creative writing—portraying the mishaps of the first day as harmless and unimportant, and stressing the collective joy of good people sailing together.

While the Reillys were waiting for Dudley to join them, Regan and Jack called over one of the waiters, who refilled their coffee cups.

"Were you here when the Lido opened at six?" Jack asked.

"Yes I was, sir."

"Did you notice the Santa Claus who would have been among your first customers?"

"He was the first customer," the waiter said,

then laughed. "I think he was one of the two Santas who were the first to arrive for the late-night buffet as well."

The Reillys looked at each other. "Doesn't that buffet start practically as soon as dinner ends?" Nora asked.

"What can I tell you? People like to eat on cruise ships. The buffet starts at eleven, but we were just setting up when the two Santas came through the door. There wasn't much out yet. They piled their plates with cheese and crackers and grapes."

"Sounds as though they missed dinner," Luke suggested.

"There were eight Santas in costume at dinner," Nora said positively. "I'm sure of it."

"Anything else I can get you?" the waiter asked.

"No, that's fine. Thank you," Regan said. As the waiter walked away, Dudley approached them. Yesterday's beaming cruise director looked as though he needed both a tranquilizer and a good night's sleep.

"Good morning," he said, his voice automatically trying to achieve his usual cheery sound as he sat down. "I feel just terrible about Mrs. Meehan—"

"Dudley," Jack interrupted, getting right to the point. "We believe that there are one, if not two, persons walking around this ship in the stolen Santa suits. Mrs. Meehan is almost positive that the Santa she saw this morning had only one bell on his cap. We want you to call a meeting of the ten Santas as soon as possible, and ask everyone who has a Santa suit to bring it to the meeting so we can confirm that none of the eight caps are missing a bell. If they all are intact, then we can be pretty sure that one of the stolen Santa suits is being used by someone on this cruise."

Dudley put his hand over his heart, as though to slow its beating. "I'll do anything you say."

Then Regan filled him in on Maggie Quirk's sighting.

"Oh, dear Lord!" Dudley sighed. "You know both Miss Quirk and Miss Pickering are roommates and are in the Readers and Writers group that is honoring Left Hook Louie. Maybe they are in on a big practical joke!"

The Reillys all shook their heads. "It would be easier for everyone if that were true," Jack said. "But we don't believe it. We're convinced that there's at least one person running around this ship who has his own agenda in mind. Dudley, I need the passenger and crew list. I'll have my office check out everyone on board."

Dudley was about to protest when Alvirah's voice called out, "Yoo-hoo!" She had a bandage over her forehead, Willy in her wake. "You won't believe what I'm going to tell you." She looked at Dudley. "I'm sure you'll hear this anyhow, so you might as well hear it now. Someone tried to kill Mr. Crater in the infirmary last night. He denies that it happened, but it must be the guy Maggie saw coming through the waiting room, the one who looks like Left Hook Louie."

Dudley moaned. "I'll get those lists for you. Right now. Immediately."

He jumped up, his feet barely touching the floor, only stopping to grab a cup of coffee on his way out of the restaurant.

# 36

At seven thirty, the ringing of Harry Crater's cell phone woke Gwendolyn and Fredericka. Ten-year-old Fredericka sat up in bed, fumbled through her drawstring purse, and grabbed the phone.

"Good morning! Fredericka speaking!" she chirped as she'd been taught in her etiquette class. "A warm greeting and then identify yourself."

"I must have dialed the wrong number," a gruff voice muttered.

A distinct click in Fredericka's ear signaled that he had hung up.

"How rude," Fredericka said to her sister. "When one dials a wrong number, a sincere apology is in order for disturbing the recipient of that call. Well, no matter, it's time for us to go down to the infirmary and cheer up Uncle Harry."

The phone rang again.

"My turn!" eight-year-old Gwendolyn cried, reaching for it. "Good morning. Gwendolyn speaking!"

Gwendolyn heard a forbidden word in her ear. "What number is this?" the caller then asked.

"I don't know. This is Uncle Harry's phone."

"Uncle Harry! Where the hell is he?"

"He's in the infirmary. We're just going to visit him now."

"What happened to him?"

"He fell and couldn't get up, so they had to carry him out of the dining room on a stretcher!"

Gwendolyn heard the same forbidden word then a sharp command: "Tell him to call his personal physician immediately!"

"Thank you, Doctor. I will relay your message. Have a nice day." She clicked off. "That doctor sounded grumpy," she told her sister.

"Most old people are grumpy," Fredericka answered. "Everyone we visit in the morning is grumpy. It's our job to make them happy, but it gets harder and harder. Let's get dressed and go."

Three minutes later, clad in matching shorts and Santa Cruise T-shirts, the girls grabbed the pictures they'd been permitted to draw for Uncle Harry last night before bedtime. Fredericka's creation depicted the sun rising over a mountain. The subject of Gwendolyn's masterpiece was a helicopter landing on a ship.

As quietly as she could, Fredericka opened the

connecting door to their parents' bedroom. Through the crack, she heard the two of them snoring. "Situation normal," she reported to her sister. "Let's go. We'll be back before they wake up."

In the infirmary, they were told by the day nurse, Allison Keane, that Mr. Crater had already returned to his room. "I don't think he wants visitors," she said.

The girls held up their pictures. "But we drew these for him!"

"How adorable," Nurse Keane said insincerely. "If you leave them here, we'll get them to him."

"But we want to see him. We love Uncle Harry!"

"I'm sorry. I can't give you his room number," Keane said firmly.

"But—" Gwendolyn started to protest.

Fredericka nudged her. "That's all right," she said. "Maybe he'll come to dinner later. Thank you, Nurse Keane." Fredericka curtseyed and they ran out the door.

"But I wanted to see Uncle Harry," Gwendolyn whined.

"Follow me." Fredericka found a house phone on a table in the passageway. She picked it up and asked for Harry Crater's room. When he answered, he sounded mad. "How are you feeling?" Fredericka asked, after properly identifying herself.

"Lousy. What do you want?"

"We drew pictures for you and want you to have them. We think they'll make you feel ever so much better."

"I'm resting. Leave me alone."

"We also have your cell phone."

It was now Fredericka's turn to hear the forbidden word. "Where are you?" Crater demanded.

"Where are *you*, Uncle Harry? We'll bring it to you."

Crater gave them his room number. A few minutes later, the girls were knocking on his door. When he opened it, it was clear he wasn't going to invite them in.

"Your doctor called!" Fredericka reported. "He wants you to call him."

"I'll bet he does," Crater mumbled as he grabbed the phone.

"Here are our drawings!" Gwendolyn said proudly. "If you have any Scotch Tape, we'll put them on the wall for you."

Crater was staring at the picture of the helicopter landing on a ship. "Who drew this?" he demanded.

"I did!" Gwendolyn said proudly. "Can I have a ride in your helicopter some day?"

"How did you know I had a helicopter?"

"After you went to the infirmary last night,

someone told Mommy and Daddy that if you got even sicker and felt like you might die or something, then your helicopter would come and pick you up. How cool!"

"Yeah, yeah. Listen, girls, I have to rest."

"We'll come back later and make sure you didn't fall again. We like to take care of sick old people."

Crater slammed the door in their faces.

The girls shrugged as they heard him turning the locks. "As Daddy would say, 'No good deed goes unpunished,' " Gwendolyn commented. "But God is watching us and smiling."

"Let's go get some coffee for Mommy and Daddy and bring it to the room," Fredericka suggested. "You know how Mommy needs her coffee in the morning."

Like a herd of elephants, the two girls thundered down the hallway, intent on performing their *second* good deed of the day.

# 37

In the living room of his suite, still clad in his blue-and-white striped pajamas, the Commodore was sitting cross-legged on the floor in an attempt to achieve inner peace. He was also bracing himself for the local news from Miami, which was about to appear on his specially equipped satellite television. At this point, inner peace was a pipe dream. He had imagined that owning the *Royal Mermaid* would bring him the solace he'd craved after three unsuccessful marriages and the passing of his beloved mother. No such luck.

The Commodore hadn't eaten a thing yet this morning. Eric had returned to the suite and told him about Alvirah Meehan's accident just as Winston was rolling in the breakfast cart. What else can possibly go wrong? the Commodore wondered. As if to answer his question, the insistently dramatic theme music of the eight o'clock news erupted from the television.

"Good morning, everyone," a handsome anchor with a Botoxed face said buoyantly, smiling at the camera. "It's December twenty-seventh. At the top of our news this morning is the widening search for Bull's-Eye Tony Pinto. There have been several reported sightings of him near the Mexican border and in Canada, but they all have turned out to be false leads. His wife, at home in their Miami mansion, keeps insisting that she's very worried about 'my Tony,' as she refers to him. She claims that she woke up yesterday morning, and he was gone. She's afraid that the stress of his upcoming trial has broken his spirit, that he may have blocked out his past life, and is wandering around in need of help. She's offered a reward of a thousand dollars for anyone with information leading to his whereabouts."

"A thousand dollars! Give me a break," the Commodore muttered. There was a knock at the door. "Come in!" he barked.

Dudley entered the room, and the Commodore motioned for him to keep his mouth shut.

"—Mrs. Pinto is having flyers passed out all over town with a photograph of Bull's-Eye holding up the Distinguished Citizen's Award he received from an unknown group."

Will I have to run away and hide to escape my troubles? the Commodore wondered glumly. I thought spending my days at sea would be so carefree and rewarding. . . .

"And now," the anchor continued, "Bianca Garcia is back to tell us more about the Santa Cruise that sailed from the Port of Miami less than twenty-four hours ago. Bianca?"

The camera swung to Bianca, who despite only getting a couple hours of sleep, had never looked more bright-eyed. In her mind she was already at Rockefeller Center hosting the *Today* show.

"Let me tell you, Adam, that is some strange cruise going on out there on the high seas, and the unexpected storm that rocked the boat last night is the least of their problems. . . ."

The Commodore started to get up, but pins and needles had developed in his legs and feet. He lost his balance and slumped clumsily to one side.

Bianca briefly recapped her earlier story. ". . . And last night after the broadcast, I heard from one of my contacts on the ship. There was more excitement. Two Santa Claus suits were stolen from a locked supply room, and a woman from the Readers and Writers group came screaming into the dining room during dinner, swearing she had seen the ghost of Left Hook Louie in the chapel! Moments ago, I heard that the famous lottery winner Alvirah Meehan slipped and fell on the deck this morning while she was trying to catch up to one of the Santas on the cruise, who was apparently running away from her. How rude! I thought there was supposed to be a bunch of do-gooders on this cruise! What's going on? Last night, I said that maybe the ghost of the original owner, Angus 'Mac' MacDuffie was on board. This woman claimed it was Left Hook Louie she saw." Pictures of the two men appeared on-screen. "Can you believe it? They were both big men who wore tartan shorts. Personally, I think it must be the ghost of MacDuffie on board.

"Let's face it, MacDuffie was eccentric. He spent all his time on that ship, even after it ended up in the backyard of the family estate he had inherited from his parents. His mother and father were out-of-control collectors. They loved anything old, from a Greek sculpture to a battered washboard, and they never threw anything away. The house was so cluttered it was considered a fire hazard. The yacht was MacDuffie's escape. He loved being at sea, enjoying the wide open space. He said he never wanted to leave that ship, and I say he's still on it!

"Which of these two men is haunting the ship? Left Hook Louie, who is being honored, or 'Mac' MacDuffie, who claimed the yacht would always be his? E-mail and let me know what you think. As my spies continue to report from the Caribbean, I'll keep you posted. . . ."

Winston had come in the room during the newscast. He'd brought the Commodore a fresh pot of coffee and two pieces of whole wheat toast, hoping his boss's appetite would return.

"She is pounding nails in my coffin!" the Commodore cried.

"There, there, sir," Winston said soothingly. "You'll see things differently after you have a cup of coffee. You know how your morning coffee always makes you optimistic and happy."

"Winston, you always know what I need," the Commodore said, glaring at the television screen, which now was showing a commercial for air freshener.

"Commodore Weed," Dudley said brightly, "I sent out a press release last night and another this morning. I'm sure they will turn everything around."

"Did you get any responses?"

"Not yet, but . . ." his voice trailed off.

The Commodore shook his head. "My poor mother," he sighed as he picked up the china coffee cup. "Her ashes must be spinning inside that box."

Dudley stared at the glass case. The silver box

with the ashes was perfectly still, but something in his mind began spinning. He turned to Winston. "Thank you, I *will* have a cup of coffee, Winston. Then if you don't mind, I'd like to talk to the Commodore in private."

Winston's body stiffened. "I'll have to go out to the galley and get you a mug," he sniffed. "I know that's what you prefer," he added condescendingly.

"Winston, you notice everything and forget nothing," the Commodore said. "I was so lucky to find you."

"Good help is always hard to find," Dudley opined.

A moment later, Winston placed a mug on the coffee table in front of Dudley, and filled it from a sterling silver coffee pot. When Dudley picked up the mug, he was sure that Winston must have run it under ice cold water. The handle was freezing. When Winston disappeared out the door, Dudley cleared his throat.

"First of all, sir, where's Eric?"

"He was here a little while ago. He got up early to check on Mr. Crater, then came back, showered and dressed, and went out again to check on the other passengers. He's such a hard worker. He told me about what happened to Mrs. Meehan, but how did the news reporter find out so quickly?

I wonder who on this ship is providing her with information. And which of our Santas was so uncaring."

Dudley could tell that Eric had not told his uncle that Dr. Gephardt believed someone had tried to suffocate Crater. He felt it was his duty to let the Commodore know. It would make the suggestion he was about to make to him more palatable. He bit the bullet and told the Commodore of the conversation Alvirah had overheard.

The Commodore was aghast. "Why didn't Eric tell me this?"

"I suppose he wanted to protect you, but my feeling is, knowledge is power."

"Eric is so good," the Commodore said. "But what if this information leaks out?"

"I can guarantee neither the Meehans nor the Reillys will say anything. I am giving Jack Reilly the passenger and crew list—he requested it. His office in New York will run the names to see if there is . . ." Dudley paused, "a troubled person among us."

"Whoever is talking to that reporter is roaming my ship right now looking for gossip," the Commodore said disgustedly. "And they're getting a free cruise! I just can't win!"

"Yes, you can! And your sainted mother is going to help you!"

"My mother?" the Commodore asked, his voice rising.

"Yes, sir. I bet that newswoman would be interested in the heartwarming story of you sending Mother Weed's ashes to the sea from this cruise ship."

"You think?"

"Absolutely. But you can't wait till tomorrow morning. We need to make tonight's news."

"But tomorrow is Mother's birthday! That's the day I wanted to bury her at sea."

"What time of day was she born?"

"At three A.M."

"Wasn't your mother born in London?"

"Yes."

"Then it was still December twenty-seventh in this part of the world."

The Commodore considered this. "You think we'd get a nice story out of her burial at sea?"

"I'm *sure* of it. Trust me, sir. More and more people are going on cruises to dispose of their beloveds' ashes. This dreadful newswoman would just love a film of the ceremony. Her viewers would definitely be intrigued. We can have the ceremony at sunset today. And believe me, you'll get a lot more people to show up in the evening than if you invite them for dawn tomorrow."

The Commodore looked over at the glass case. "What do you think, Mother?" he asked.

Dudley almost expected the box to spring open and a head to pop out.

"You say more people would attend?" the Commodore asked Dudley.

"Many more, sir. We'll have the ceremony out on deck at sunset. Your remarks will be poignant and brief, then we will sing hymns and finally have a champagne toast after you drop Mother Weed's remains overboard."

The Commodore hesitated. "Isn't this exploiting my mother's burial for my own gain?"

"She's your mother," Dudley answered quickly. "She'd be so happy to know she was helping you out of this mess."

The Commodore considered that. "I know she would," he said. "She was so unselfish. You said we should have the ceremony out on deck. What about that lovely chapel I built for just such a purpose?"

"It's too small. I'm going to make sure everyone on board shows up this evening. We'll put up notices, make announcements over the loudspeaker, and at lunchtime when everyone is together we'll go from table to table, reminding our guests that they won't want to miss the ceremony."

"All right, Dudley. I think I'll spend the day

alone with Mother. I only have nine hours left with her and—" his voice caught, "I'd like to make the most of them."

"You really *should* be at lunch, sir. Your presence is a statement that all is well."

"You're right again, Dudley." The Commodore stood up. "High time I showered and dressed. Even when I was a lad, Mother never liked it when I lounged around in my pajamas."

"I'm on my way to prepare the announcements and alert the staff." Dudley said. "I'll disturb you only if it's absolutely necessary."

# 38

Crater was frantic. It was bad enough that someone had tried to kill him, and he was greatly relieved that those annoying kids had returned his cell phone, but now his briefcase with all the cash and his several passports was missing.

Someone had definitely been in his room when he was gone! How could he report the theft? If someone was just after the cash and then tossed the briefcase, he'd be better not having people look for it. Anyone who saw all the passports would know he was up to no good. But more important, would whoever had tried to kill him try again?

Crater placed a call to his henchman and tersely explained why the kids had the phone. "You're still set to arrive at dawn tomorrow?" he asked. "I certainly won't have a problem faking a medical emergency now."

"We're set to go," he was reassured. "We've seen

television reports about problems on that ship. Do you think it will affect our mission?"

"So someone thought she saw a ghost!" Crater snapped. "Forget it. That's the last thing I'm worried about. You guys better be ready to move fast when you land on board tomorrow morning. We won't have much time. And we'll be a lot better off if nobody gets hurt. Don't screw up," he warned.

Crater thought he could be sure of the personal loyalty of the three men who would be arriving in the helicopter. After a moment's debate with himself, he decided to say nothing about the attempt on his life. The guys who were coming had no idea that he wasn't the big boss on this job. They didn't have a clue that she even existed.

And that's the way she wanted it, he reminded himself. He was getting a big enough piece of the action to go along with her wishes. He just wanted this job to be over with, to collect his pay, and ring in the New Year on dry land.

He turned on the television and caught a piece on the news feed about Bull's-Eye Tony Pinto and the false sightings of him in Canada and Mexico. Crater's mouth went dry at the sight of Pinto filling the screen.

The words his would-be killer had whispered ran through his head: "This is what you deserve."

Bull's-Eye swore he'd get me after I ratted on his father, Crater remembered. It occurred to him that there was a strong resemblance between Bull's-Eye and that writer whose posters were plastered all over the ship. Wait a minute, he thought. When I was working with Pinto Senior didn't I hear something about his wife's brother being a boxer who started writing after he retired? I think so. . . .

A torrent of thoughts ran through his head. That woman screaming that she'd seen the writer in the chapel, someone trying to kill me; Bull's-Eye looks a lot like the pictures of that writer, and there's a good chance they're related. . . .

"This is what you deserve," echoed in his head.

Crater suddenly felt sick to his stomach. The news people had it straight. Bull's-Eye wasn't in Canada or Mexico.

Crater knew in his bones that Bull's-Eye, the man who had sworn to track him down, was hiding somewhere on this ship.

# 39

The Lido was quickly filling up with guests. Afraid of being overheard, the Reillys and Meehans had gone to Alvirah and Willy's cabin so that they could talk and Alvirah could lie down on her bed.

"I'm safer here than in that infirmary," Alvirah declared, "but who knows if anyone is safe on this ship? I'm just sorry I got you all into this."

"No, you're not, Alvirah," Nora said, smiling.

"You attract trouble, and you enjoy it," Luke agreed.

"I'll admit it makes me feel alive," Alvirah said, then wished she hadn't nodded, as a sharp pain shot across her forehead. "I always preferred working in houses for people who were a little off," she declared. "It was so much more interesting than just cleaning up after your average slob."

"You're not even safe with Santa Claus," Luke commented.

Alvirah cleared her throat, anxious to get down to business. "I know we don't have proof, but it sounds as if someone really tried to kill Crater. Why him, and why is he denying it? If it happened, that means there's a would-be killer on this ship, who might strike again. The thing is, you can't tap someone on the shoulder and ask if they tried to suffocate Crater."

"Dudley promised he'd get me the passenger and crew list right away," Jack said. "My office will have it checked out in a couple of hours. They'll find out if there's anyone of interest on the list, and we'll see what Crater's all about."

"Something else," Alvirah said. Trying to ignore the aching in her head, she pulled open the drawer and reached for the deck of cards. She explained how she had discovered the peculiar markings on the royal cards in the deck and what happened when you held them up to the mirror. "Willy found the cards in the drawer of this room, which was Eric's, but Eric didn't seem to know anything about them when we tried to return the cards to him. I think they might be a clue to whatever's going on around here."

Alvirah's phone rang. It was Dudley. Alvirah put him on speakerphone. "I'm meeting all the Santas in fifteen minutes in my office and I have the passenger and crew list!"

"Jack and I will be right there," Regan said.

"Okay." Dudley hung up.

Jack picked up the deck of cards as they got ready to leave Alvirah's cabin. "My bet is that these belong to a card shark. I'll see if I can check those symbols out. There's a guy in my office who specializes in gambling fraud and might have an idea of what these numbers mean, if anything."

Alvirah wanted to go with Reagan and Jack but knew she would be voted down if she made the suggestion. With regret, she watched them file out the door.

"I'll keep my thinking cap on," she called after them. "I can promise you that."

# 40

The ten Santas, eight of them in costume, were standing shoulder to shoulder in Dudley's small office. It was easy to do a quick check of the outfits. All eight caps were fully belled. The story of Alvirah's accident had spread quickly and the fact that she had been ignored by someone in a Santa outfit had united the Santas in righteous indignation, even Bobby Grimes.

"That guy's giving the rest of us a bad name," he said piously. "Like I said last night, we'd all better be on the lookout."

Dudley glanced at Jack, who took over. "We need your help," Jack explained. "We all agree that whoever has those outfits is either a passenger or a crew member who probably has some sort of practical joke agenda. However, as we've seen with Mrs. Meehan, jokes can cause accidents. The ten of you can be very helpful, provided what we're saying here doesn't go out of this room. For the rest of the trip, please keep your eyes peeled for a Santa who only has one bell on his cap. We need to find him."

"With my luck, the bell's going to fall off my cap," Bobby Grimes complained.

"We know who you are," Jack assured him with a smile.

"Who would do this?" Nelson asked rhetorically.

Dudley shrugged. "Your job as Santa Claus was to find out what people wanted for Christmas. The job we're giving you today is to help us catch this troublemaker."

"The problem is you'd have to see the back of this Santa's head to notice how many bells he has on his cap," Ted Cannon observed.

"We thought of that," Dudley said. "That's why I'm giving you the *Royal Mermaid* souvenir pins now, instead of as a good-bye present at the end of the cruise. Wear them on the front of your Santa Claus jackets and that will identify you as an official Santa Cruise Santa Claus."

"We've all been watching television," Nelson said, shaking his head. "This ship has certainly been getting a lot of attention."

"Mountains out of mole hills," Dudley replied airily. "And it all comes back to our practical joker."

"Was the waiter who jumped overboard a practical joker?" one of the Santas asked. "Who are his friends? Maybe one of them is pulling this."

"That's my job," Jack said. "We're checking him out."

"I do want to remind you that you are the Commodore's special guests on this trip," Dudley said earnestly. "I'll be perfectly honest. The unfavorable publicity could mean the end of the Commodore's dream—this ship. On the other hand, if you help to create an atmosphere of good feeling among the passengers, you really will be giving the Commodore the one thing he has always wanted in life—the chance to run a successful cruise ship, on which people can forget their troubles and be happy."

Well done, Dudley, Regan thought.

"One more very important matter," Dudley said. "The Commodore was very close to his mother. Her ashes are on board. We are going to have a memorial service for her at sunset tonight on the Promenade Deck. All passengers will be asked to attend. There will be a brief ceremony, a few hymns sung, the Commodore will say good-bye to his mother as he lovingly drops the box with her ashes over the railing, then we'll share a champagne toast."

"Why are her ashes going to be thrown over in

a box? I thought you just sprinkle them into the breeze," Grimes asked with a frown.

"That's environmentally unhealthy," Nelson explained. "They only do that in the movies. My therapist told me one of his patients wanted to scatter his father's ashes near all the bars he used to frequent, but needless to say the City of New York told him to go jump in a lake with his father's ashes."

"As long as they were still in a box," someone added.

"I would like to have a Santa escort for the Commodore tonight," Dudley continued. "Eight of you in uniform will accompany Commodore Weed and his mother as they travel from his suite to the chapel for a brief prayer, then down the companionway, and out onto the Promenade Deck where the rest of the passengers and crew will be waiting. Who would like to be in the procession?"

Ten hands shot up.

Dudley smiled. "We'll draw straws. And who knows? If we catch the Santa-suit thieves today, then you'll *all* be in the procession."

# 41

Highbridge and Bull's-Eye, aware of their close call, and that every passing minute was bringing them closer to freedom on Fishbowl Island, sat hunched under the altar in the chapel. Their hands clasped around their knees, they kept adjusting their bodies, trying to find a comfortable place to rest. There was none.

It was hard to keep perfectly quiet. Bull's-Eye's normally heavy breathing seemed outrageously loud to a nervous Highbridge. The damp cold of Bull's-Eye's suit was penetrating his body and making him both chilled and itchy. Even though they had both unhooked their beards, they kept them on their laps to be able to refasten them in an instant. Not that that would do either of us any good, Highbridge thought. Suppose someone comes in and lifts this cloth. What are we supposed to do? Pretend we're playing hide-and-seek?

Tired and realizing how totally vulnerable they

were in this public space, they hoped against hope that no one would find them before Eric showed up and brought them to the relative security of his cabin.

At nine thirty, when they heard the door of the chapel open, they both stiffened. Bull's-Eye almost stopped breathing.

"Here we are, Mother," they heard a male voice say.

But there was no response.

Footsteps coming down the aisle, getting closer and closer to the altar, made both men break into a cold sweat. The footsteps stopped at what must have been the first or second row, and the faint squeak suggested someone sat down.

"This is a lovely chapel, isn't it, Mother?"

Again no response. Bull's-Eye and Highbridge looked at each other dumbfounded.

"I was going to drop you overboard at dawn tomorrow, but we're moving up the ceremony to sunset tonight. I hope you don't mind. Dudley says you won't—that that's what mothers are for— helping out in time of need. We've been having a lot of trouble since we set sail. I swear if I find whoever stole those Santa suits, I'll thrash them within an inch of their lives. Sorry, Mother, I know I shouldn't talk that way. I keep thinking of all the trips we took together. Remember when your hat blew off on the crossing of the old *Queen Elizabeth?* Someone from an upper deck who saw the hat floating away was afraid you were still wearing it and shouted, 'Lady overboard!' "

The Commodore laughed tenderly. "That's when you said you wanted the sea to be your final resting place. I made you a promise that you would be buried at sea. Today—I'm fulfilling that promise—"

For five minutes the Commodore sat quietly, the hammered silver box in his lap, fond memories of his mother running through his mind. He got up to leave just as the chapel door opened. The woman who had been screaming about seeing Left Hook Louie last night was standing before him.

"Commodore Weed! I'm so glad you're here. I was afraid to come back to the chapel, but they say you should face your fears. That's what I was doing, and I'm lucky enough to find you here as well."

"My pleasure," the Commodore said stiffly.

It was obvious to Ivy that he resented the uproar she had created. "I can tell that you are mad at me, Commodore Weed, and I can certainly understand, but I'm telling you I did see someone here in the chapel last night. I wasn't trying to cause trouble." Ivy's voice started to tremble.

Bull's-Eye and Highbridge both held their breath. Please God, Highbridge thought, don't let her start looking under the altar.

"This cruise is the nicest thing that ever happened to me in my whole life," Ivy continued. "The ship is so beautiful, the food is wonderful, the people are so exciting. I know you're responsible for all this, and I know this ship is your dream, and I wouldn't want to do anything to destroy your dream."

Despite himself, the Commodore was touched. "Thank you, Miss Pickering. I appreciate your sentiments. I haven't felt much gratitude, and I must say it hurts." He looked closely at her. "There, there, you mustn't cry now."

Ivy wiped her eyes and became aware of the object in the Commodore's hands. "That's a beautiful jewelry case you have there. My mother has one almost exactly like it."

The Commodore grabbed her hand. "Your *mother?*" he said, his voice a whisper. He held up the box. "My mother's ashes are resting in this box. You say your mother has one like it?"

"Yes, my Papa bought it for her in a museum shop on their honeymoon. She still has it on the dresser at home."

The door opened again. This time it was Eric, looking flustered and out of breath. He stared at them, stared at the altar, then back at Ivy and his uncle. He tried to pull himself together. "Uncle Randolph, I just heard about your new plans for Grandma." With his usual lack of courtesy, he ignored Ivy. "It will be very special."

Ivy looked questioningly at the Commodore. It was obvious she hadn't heard about the sunset ceremony.

The Commodore touched her hand again. "Would you care to join me for a cup of tea in my suite and I'll explain?" he asked. He paused. "Please," he added.

The Commodore and Ivy left Eric in the chapel. Not knowing what he would find, he ran up to the altar, bent down, and lifted the cloth.

"Your uncle sounds like a nutcase," Bull's-Eye muttered. Then he released the sneeze he'd been holding back.

# 42

There's no question I'm not as tough as I used to be, Alvirah admitted to herself. Her head was really aching, and now the rest of her body was letting her know that she'd taken a pretty good tumble. At her insistence, Willy had gone down to the gym where he had a treadmill reserved for ten o'clock. By then, Winston had brought Alvirah tea, fruit, and toast, and even Willy admitted that aside from the bandage and goose-egg bump on her forehead, she did seem to be okay. Alvirah said, "Willy, be on your way. I really do have to put my thinking cap on. But first turn on the television. I'd like to see what's going on in the outside world."

"Okay," Willy agreed. "I'll be back in less than an hour. That guy Winston is always around. If you feel just a little bit funny, please ring for him."

The state of the world hadn't changed much in the twenty-four hours since she'd seen a broadcast. It was a holiday week, and most of the politicians had taken time off from insulting each other. The day-after-Christmas sales in retail stores had broken records. On the other hand, more gifts had been returned this year than had been brought back in the last ten years. Shows how much junk people give just to get their gift buying out of the way, Alvirah thought. She was just starting to doze off when the picture of Bull's-Eye Tony Pinto came across the screen.

"Blessed Mother!" Alvirah murmured. She remembered reading about him when he lived in New York and was often in the headlines of the *Post* and the *Daily News*. I loved to read up on him, she admitted to herself. He was so colorful. He spent some time in prison for small stuff, but they could never get him on any of the big charges. Everybody knows he's a killer. His reputation was that he got rid of anyone who was in his way. . . .

"Coming up," the newscaster said, "the latest on the all-out manhunt for mobster Bull's-Eye Tony Pinto, who disappeared from his home in Miami yesterday. But first this . . ."

Alvirah ignored the four fifteen-second commercials for various prescription drugs, her mind totally focused on the startling resemblance between Tony Pinto and Left Hook Louie.

"Is it possible?" she wondered aloud. "I think

it's *more* than possible," she concluded. She had to talk to Regan and Jack. If Bull's-Eye is on this ship trying to make his way to freedom, has he already attempted a murder? He was always accused of murder, never convicted. And what would make him want to kill Crater? And if he did try to kill him, who's next?

She snapped on her microphone. "Pinto lives in Miami. He's desperate to get out of the country. This ship was sailing from Miami the same day he disappeared. He looks like that writer guy in the posters, the same guy Ivy and Maggie thought they saw. But if he is on board, someone has to have helped him get here, and someone is hiding him now. Maybe the same person who stole the Santa suits. But who?"

A suspicion that was rapidly becoming a certainty had formed in Alvirah's mind. "I felt from minute one that there was something odd about that nephew, Eric," she said. "He's nervous. I'm beginning to think he may have something big to hide." At that moment, her phone rang. It was Eric.

"Mrs. Meehan, I do hope you're feeling better."

"Yes, I am."

"That deck of cards Mr. Meehan showed me last night. It completely slipped my mind. One of the other officers stopped by to have a drink with me the night before you boarded. They belong to him. He must have put them down, and when we went out to dinner, I bet Winston put them in my drawer, assuming they were mine. May I stop by and pick them up?"

Alvirah didn't believe him for a minute. "I'm lying down and Willy's not here," she said. "Let me call you back. Or if you give us the name of the officer, Willy would be happy to get them back to him."

"That won't be necessary. He'll be off duty until tonight. I'll come by for them later."

I'll bet you will, Alvirah thought as she hung up the phone to make sure the connection was broken. Wait till I tell Jack and Regan, she exulted as she picked up the phone again and began to dial.

# 43

After the morning newscast, Bianca had been pleased with the number of e-mails she had received. I've got to keep it up, she thought. Until she could get more information on what was happening on the ship from her contacts, she had to find a way to keep the story going. Otherwise, she knew that even if something startling surfaced in a couple of days, people would already have lost interest.

Her viewers were voting on who was the ghost. Most thought it was Mac. Then one e-mail made her gasp as she read it.

*Dear Bianca,*

*When MacDuffie died a few years ago, my mother and I went to the estate sale. All the antique dealers were there, combing over the stuff. It was mostly a bunch of junk! But my* mother and I can't resist a bargain and we bought a few pieces of furniture and several cartons of papers and magazines. Well, what did we find but the journal MacDuffie kept of his last years on that yacht! Can you believe that he wrote that his father had squandered much of the family fortune by buying a famous jewelry box that he knew had been stolen from a museum? He claimed it had been given to Cleopatra by Marc Antony, and was priceless. I ask you! What was he smoking?

Mac wrote that he couldn't sell the box because it would destroy the family name, and anyhow the museum would claim it back. Here's a direct quote: "So I sit on my yacht and think of five thousand years ago when a handsome Roman presented it to a young queen." Yeah, and my mother and I are the Gabor sisters!!!

Anyhow, thought you'd be interested. My vote is that Mac's haunting that ship, and maybe Cleopatra's on board, too. By the way, my mother and I checked the list of items for sale and there was no jewelry box belonging to Cleopatra on it!

> Your fan,
> Kimmie Keating

Perfect! Bianca thought. Gleefully, she reread the e-mail.

If there was anything more compelling than a story about a ghost, it was one about a missing treasure.

# 44

"$M$aking a list, checking it twice," Dudley sang, in a feeble attempt to lighten the atmosphere after the Santas had left his office.

Jack placed a call to his assistant, Keith. "The cruise director is e-mailing you the passenger and crew list right now," he explained. "Check everyone out, but begin with Harry Crater—he's a passenger. I'll talk to you in a few minutes from my room." Jack hung up, turned to Dudley and asked, "How did Crater end up on this ship?"

"A nurse wrote me about all the good he had done and said that he was very ill, and this would be his last cruise." Dudley pulled out a file and handed Jack the letter. It listed the many contributions Crater had supposedly made in the last year.

"Could you make a copy of that for us?" Regan asked.

"Of course."

When Regan and Jack left Dudley's office, passenger and crew lists in hand, they found Ted Cannon waiting for them in the corridor.

"I didn't want to say anything in front of the others," he told them, "but something occurred that I thought you might want to know. It might be nothing . . ."

"What is it?" Regan asked.

"That fellow Harry Crater, who's in the infirmary. I know he's traveling alone. When I went to bed last night, I heard noise coming from his room. The television was on, and I heard people talking and drawers opening and closing. I had seen him being carried off, after he fell at dinner, and I thought he must have been brought back to his room. Apparently not. It just seemed odd, and I thought you might want to know."

"These things are always good to know," Jack said.

"Have they found out who it was Maggie saw in the waiting room?" Ted asked.

"Not that we know of," Regan told him.

"I have to admit it bothers me to think that Maggie was alone in that waiting room in the middle of the night when some unknown character came wandering through."

He's right, Regan thought. And he doesn't even know that the man might have tried to suffocate Crater. Maggie could have been in big trouble, especially if there wasn't any motive for the attempted murder and the intruder was simply deranged. "It is scary to think that she was alone with that guy," she agreed.

"I told Maggie that if Ivy starts to feel sick in the middle of the night again, she's to call me and not go anywhere alone," he said firmly. "I know you're reviewing the passenger and crew list. If I can help you in any way, give me a call. Otherwise I'll see you later." With a wave of his hand, he turned and headed down the corridor.

"I think he's got a crush on Maggie," Regan observed.

"He does. I feel dishonest not telling him Maggie might have been face-to-face with a would-be killer."

"Me too," Regan said.

They were walking past a poster of Left Hook Louie that had been taped to the wall of the corridor. They stopped to examine it, both thinking of the photograph of the missing Tony Pinto they'd seen on television.

"It's certainly possible," Jack said quietly, after a pause.

Regan knew exactly what he meant.

When they reached their cabin, the phone was ringing. Regan ran to pick it up. It was Alvirah.

"Regan, it's a good thing I stayed here. I have two things to report. I was watching the news, and there's a mobster who's missing who—"

"Bull's-Eye Tony Pinto," Regan interrupted. "I know what you're going to say, and Jack and I have been thinking along the same lines. We joked about it last night, but it's not a joke anymore."

"Two and two makes four," Alvirah said. "He was trying to get out of the country. He lives in Miami. He has been missing since the day our ship sailed, and two people on this cruise claim to have seen someone who looks just like him. And they didn't see him out on deck sunning himself. The other thing I want to tell you," she went on without waiting for a comment from Regan, "is that Eric, the nephew, just called with a phony-baloney story about that deck of cards belonging to one of the officers on the ship, and how he wanted to come by and pick them up. I told him Willy would be happy to deliver the cards to the officer, but of course that nonexistent officer was off duty."

"Hold on, Alvirah." Regan told Jack Eric's tall story about the cards. Jack took the phone from her.

"Alvirah, I'll get pictures of the cards sent to the office right away, then I'll get them back to you. If Eric is involved in *any way* with the problems on this ship, we don't want to tip our hand to him. I'll tell my office to look at his background carefully."

As soon as they had hung up, Jack photographed the backs of the royal cards with his digital camera, e-mailed them to his office, and called Keith. While he was on the phone, Regan took the cards, went into the bathroom, held them up to the magnifying mirror, and jotted down the numbers. If we're going to give these cards back to Eric, she thought, I want to be sure we have a copy of the information on them.

She went back into the bedroom. Jack had just hung up the phone. "Keith promised to get back to me as quickly as possible."

"I have an idea," Regan said. "Let's walk around this ship for a while. If Ivy, Maggie, and Alvirah all managed to run into strange characters without trying, maybe we'll get lucky when we *are* trying. Anyhow, I'd like to get some fresh air."

"Fine with me. Let's get cleaned up and see what's out there. This isn't *that* big a ship. If Tony Pinto is on board, he's not far away."

Jack's cell phone rang. He raised his eyebrows questioningly as he answered it. The caller was Regan's best friend Kit. "Hey, Kit," he said. "How's it going?"

"Still looking for a date for New Year's Eve. I went to a party in Greenwich last night hoping I might find someone who doesn't have plans, either. Needless to say, it didn't happen. But I did get some scoop I thought you guys might enjoy."

"Hold on, Kit. I'll put your buddy on."

Regan took the phone. "I could hear what you were saying to Jack. Don't worry about New Year's Eve. It's always a terrible night anyway."

"I know. But that doesn't mean I'm not going to worry about it all week. But get *this!* I went to my friend Donna's annual post-Christmas party last night in Greenwich. All anyone was talking about was this guy Highbridge, who cheated so many investors, including a lot of people at the party. As you may have heard, he's now on the run. Everyone assumes he headed to the Caribbean. So I thought of you. And there's more! One of the women at the party said Highbridge's ex-girlfriend Lindsay, who'd tried to get friendly with a lot of the people Highbridge knew in Greenwich, claimed that he phoned her yesterday. The number was blocked, but a radio was blasting in the background. She was sure she heard someone announce the local temperature in Miami."

"You're kidding!" Regan said. "They must have had a bad breakup if she's telling people about his call."

"She's out in Aspen with her new beau and told people about the phone call late last night when she was out clubbing. I guess she'd had a few drinks by then. The sister of one of the girls at the party is out in Aspen. She and her husband were within earshot when Lindsay was blabbering on about Highbridge."

"Was there any talk of Lindsay going to the police with that story?"

"No. Now she's denying she ever said anything about Highbridge. Anyway, I thought you'd be interested since you're in the Caribbean and sailed from Miami."

"I am interested," Regan said. "You never met Highbridge at any of Donna's parties, did you?"

"I met him once, about five or six years ago."

"What was your impression of him?"

"Tall, boring, and full of himself."

"I guess he didn't ask for your number," Regan chuckled.

"How did you know?" Kit laughed. "I think when he realized I didn't have any money he could steal, he moved on."

After Regan hung up, they decided Jack should call his office one more time.

"Keith," Jack said to his assistant, "this is probably a long shot, but see if you can find any connection at all between Bull's-Eye Pinto and Barron Highbridge." He paused. "Besides the fact that they're both on the run."

# 45

At the insistence of their mother, Fredericka and Gwendolyn had gone for a swim in the pool. "A sound mind in a sound body," Eldona trilled as she sat at the water's edge, her feet dangling in the pool, two pages of next year's Christmas newsletter already written. "Here we are on the maiden voyage of the *Royal Mermaid*, and the kindliness of my girls is already the talk of the ship. . . ."

When the girls had finished their required laps, they had a water fight, which succeeded in splashing people sunning in deck chairs around the pool. "The energy of the young gladdens the heart," Eldona continued as she wiped her glasses.

Word of the Commodore's mother's service was being spread by the stewards who were already serving Bloody Marys and Margaritas. Needless to say, Fredericka and Gwendolyn got wind of the impending ceremony. They climbed out of the pool.

"Mommy," Fredericka said breathlessly. "Did you hear about the sunset service?"

"Yes, dear. And you may attend. It will be very beautiful."

"Maybe we can sing at it, like we do in church."

Eldona's eyes glistened with tenderness. "What a lovely idea. I think the Commodore would appreciate that. But you should make sure. Why don't you run and put on a play outfit and ask him yourselves?"

"Yeaaaahhhhhhhhh." The two girls clapped hands and jumped up and down. "Where did Daddy go? Let's tell Daddy!"

"Over there in the corner," Eldona pointed to her husband, who was sprawled on a lounge chair, a magazine covering his face. "He moved to the shade. You know how careful he is of his health. He'll be so happy to hear about your thoughtfulness."

"I've got a better idea, Mommy. Let's make it a surprise for him when we sing tonight."

"Whatever you want, darlings. Run along now."

The Commodore and Ivy were on their third cup of English Breakfast tea. He had tenderly placed the silver chest with his mother's ashes on the coffee table. When Winston brought in the tray with the teapot, strainer, cups, and saucers, he had set it on the table, then started to pick up the box. The Commodore had sternly reprimanded him. "That is only for my hands, Winston. Leave it there. Mother always enjoyed a cup of tea."

"My mother loves tea, too," Ivy said. It was a thrill to be in the Commodore's suite. When she first met him, she had been intimidated. He was such an imposing, rugged *manly* man. The kind of man her mother would call "a fine, big fellow." But sitting talking to Commodore Weed made her realize that he was a real softie inside, that like so many people, he was someone who wanted to be loved.

Now, as the Commodore refilled her cup, he said, "Ivy, as I told you in the chapel, you make me feel so good about this cruise." He laughed. "I had three ex-wives who married me for what they perceived I could give them. My last wife, Reeney, and I are actually still quite friendly—"

Ivy felt a pang of jealousy.

"—but we just couldn't agree on so many things. She wanted to go antiquing all the time. She fancied she had an eye for value, which I can assure you she did not. But the worst thing was she hated boating—"

"I *love* boating," Ivy cried.

"Me, too. But Reeney helped with a lot of things, I must admit. She's a great organizer. She helped me decorate the house in Miami that I bought after our divorce. She even helped me find Winston. She told me I didn't need another wife, I needed a butler. Someone who wanted to take care of me."

Ivy had to clamp her lips together to keep from blurting out, "I'd *love* to take care of you!"

"You say you've never been married, Ivy?" the Commodore asked her, a tone of wonder in his voice, unconsciously calling her by her first name. "An attractive lady like you?"

Ivy felt a warm glow. She was having such a wonderful time! She didn't want it to end. She started to murmur, "Ohhhhh, thank you," when a loud banging at the door startled them both.

"What now?" the Commodore asked, as he got up and impatiently crossed the room and opened the door.

Fredericka and Gwendolyn curtseyed to him. "Good morning, Commodore Weed." Without being invited, they dashed past him into the room. "Good morning, Ma'am," they said to Ivy, curtseying again.

"Hello, girls," Ivy said, thinking the curtsey was the ultimate irony since the two of them had forced their way in.

"Ohhh, how pretty," Fredericka said as she reached to pick up the silver chest.

Ivy was too quick for her. Her hand clamped over it. "That's the Commodore's," she said firmly.

The Commodore had almost passed out at the sight of his mother's ashes being jostled by this pushy child. "What can I do for you girls?" he asked, trying to conceal his feelings.

"We heard about the special service for your Mommy tonight. We'd love to sing a special song," Fredericka explained.

"We're in the children's choir at home," Gwendolyn chimed in.

God help me, the Commodore thought.

"There's a song that we learned in school that we thought would be perfect. We just changed one word. 'My *Mommy* lies over the ocean! My *Mommy* lies over the sea . . .'"

Ivy watched them in disbelief.

"Thank you," the Commodore said. "That would be very nice. Perhaps at the end of the service. Now go practice," he said, his voice husky.

"Goody!" they cried. "We'll tell everyone on the

ship they have to come!" They ran out the door.

Gwendolyn turned to Fredericka. "Now let's go see how Uncle Harry is. We'll tell him about the service. We can reserve a seat for him and help him get to the deck. I'm sure he won't want to miss it."

# 46

The only time Eric had left the chapel all morning was to run outside and use the house phone to call Alvirah Meehan to ask if he could pick up the cards. Eric knew that he could not leave the chapel unguarded until lunchtime, when he could sneak Bull's-Eye and Highbridge into his room in his uncle's suite. Once he got them there, they could hide safely in the closet until four A.M. tomorrow morning.

At that point, the plan was that Eric would lead the two men to the lowest outside deck where they'd blow up the inflatable dinghy Eric had hidden on board, toss it over, and wearing life jackets, they'd jump in after it. Their people would be hovering nearby, ready to rescue the men when the *Royal Mermaid* was a safe distance away. I wouldn't want to be in their shoes—their *wet* shoes—Eric thought, but it's better than spending a good part of your life in prison.

As he sat in the third pew, he had plenty of time to worry about what would happen if Bull's-Eye and Highbridge were discovered. Highbridge was the type who cleared his well-bred throat unconsciously, a sound that reverberated through the still chapel. But it had only happened once. Eric had run up the aisle to shush him, but Bull's-Eye had already clasped a pudgy hand over Highbridge's mouth and warned him that he'd kill him if he did it again. Eric didn't doubt for a moment that it was a serious threat. Bull's-Eye Pinto was a *killer*, first and foremost.

Eric was counting the minutes until twelve o'clock, when he knew his uncle would go down to lunch. At eleven, a steward came in to dust and vacuum the chapel.

"That won't be necessary," Eric said.

"But I was instructed to make the chapel sparkle. People may want to come here before your grandmother's service."

"Wait until this afternoon to clean," Eric ordered. "And bring some fresh flowers for the altar."

"Of course."

Eric felt beads of perspiration on his forehead. The steward would undoubtedly have lifted the altar cloth to vacuum. He could only imagine the brush of the vacuum cleaner hitting Bull's-Eye.

At twelve fifteen, the Commodore opened the chapel door and stood in the doorway. "What a surprise to find you here," he said.

"I just stopped by to say a prayer for Grandma. She is so in my thoughts today."

"Oh, how I share that with you! But come now. I want you to join me for lunch. Ivy—I mean, Miss Pickering—will also be at the table. A very sweet woman indeed."

Eric knew that was a warning not to ignore Ivy again. "I'll take a moment to freshen up," he said. He walked with the Commodore to the elevator bank, pushed the DOWN button, and waited until he had seen the back of his uncle's head before he dashed down the corridor. As he feared, he bumped into Winston, who was on his way to his room. He had a two-hour break at lunchtime.

"Anything I can get you before I leave?" Winston asked.

"No, I'll be heading to the dining room in a few minutes."

Eric opened the door of the suite and stood just inside until he was sure Winston was gone. Then he hurried back to the chapel. "Come on. I'm going to stand outside the Meehans' door. If they come out, I'll divert them. You make a dash for the suite—quietly, if that's possible. The door is open."

The precaution wasn't necessary. The two felons entered the suite undetected. Eric followed them in. "We can't take any chances. Grab whatever drinks and snacks you want from my refrigerator. Then get in the closet and *stay* there. I'll be back as soon as I can."

"Don't forget to get my cards," Bull's-Eye warned him.

Eric splashed water on his face and combed his hair. This time when he left the suite, Alvirah and Willy were coming out of their stateroom.

"Hello," he called to them. "Is it okay if I grab those cards before you close your door?"

Alvirah admired the way Willy could think on his feet. "Eric, do you mind waiting until after lunch? I'm in the midst of a game of solitaire and I'm actually winning," he joked.

Eric tried to laugh. "Oh sure. This afternoon would be fine."

But it didn't *feel* fine. There was something wrong, he could tell. They knew he wanted the cards back, so why had Willy started another stupid game of solitaire?

He didn't believe the story, but there was nothing he could do about it.

The memory of Alvirah saying she was a good amateur sleuth nagged at him as they rode down in the elevator together.

# 47

Harry Crater sat in the easy chair in his state-room, his nerves jangling. The bruises on his neck had turned dark purple, and spread to the tissue around them like wine stains. The nightmare that had turned into reality kept playing on his mind. I'll stay in my cabin and have my meals sent in, he told himself. I only have until daybreak. Nobody can come in here while I have the door double-locked.

He had devoured most of the breakfast he had ordered. The sight of the empty plate, which had contained scrambled eggs and bacon, was another reminder that he was lucky to be alive to have eaten breakfast this morning. He was worried about Bull's-Eye, and in his gut he was sure that the big boss had placed someone else on the ship. Who was it? And what would he or she do after the helicopter landed?

He reached for the coffee pot, hoping there

were a few sips remaining. A staccato banging at the door startled him, so much that his hand jerked and the last of the coffee ended up on the tray.

"Uncle Harry!"

"I'm in bed, go away."

"We have an invitation for you!"

"For what?" he called.

"We're going to sing at the ceremony when the Commodore throws his mother's ashes into the sea."

Harry paled. He got up and hurried to open the door.

Gwendolyn and Fredericka beamed at him. "We just visited the Commodore," they said, interrupting each other to convey the important news. "You have to come tonight. You *have* to. We're going to sing. We'll come and get you. We'll have a chair for you."

"He's throwing his mother's ashes into the sea tonight? I think you mean sunrise. Tomorrow morning."

"Tonight!" said Fredericka firmly. "It's tonight."

"I'll be there." He spat out the words, shut the door, and raced to get his cell phone. When the call went through he snapped, "We've got to move up the plan. You've been keeping up with us, I trust. How far away are you now?"

"We're on Shark Island," was the reply. "It's two hours flight time. We have an extra tank of fuel to get us back here, if we need to leave now."

"Get moving! The Commodore has moved up the ceremony. It's taking place at sunset. I knew we shouldn't have counted on him to wait for his mother's birthday. We can't take a chance that he'll change the time again. Once you're here, I'll say that I don't want to leave until after the service."

He added sarcastically, "The Commodore will be so touched. You three 'medics' can be the honor guard surrounding my wheelchair." He listened. "Don't tell *me* to take it easy. Someone tried to *kill* me last night. And I'm pretty sure I know who it was."

He slammed down the phone.

# 48

The Oklahoma Readers and Writers seminar had been in full swing since nine A.M. Groups had lively discussions about the art of mystery writing, dating back to such famous writers as Sir Arthur Conan Doyle and Dame Agatha Christie.

At eleven thirty, Bosley P. Brevers, the author of an exhaustive biography of Left Hook Louie, was scheduled to lecture on his favorite subject, and show slides of Louie's life in the small theater near the dining salon.

Regan and Jack had run into Nora and Luke on the deck, and they'd all decided to attend. Regan had confided to her parents their growing suspicion that Tony Pinto might be a stowaway on the ship.

In the audience, they spotted Ivy Pickering and Maggie Quirk sitting a little to the left in the row behind them. Regan's eyebrows shot up. Ivy, who had seemed like the type who never bothered with so much as dabbing powder on her nose, was wearing becoming makeup and a blue linen jacket that set off her cornflower blue eyes. What a difference from the way she had looked last night when she'd come screaming into the dining room, Regan thought.

On the stage, Brevers was being introduced. The director of the seminar praised Brevers's five years of scholarly research on his subject and noted he was also the principal of an award-winning high school at the time he was working on the book. Brevers, a small man in his mid-sixties, with a slight frame and white hair, approached the lectern. He made the usual comments about how honored he was to speak and what a thrill it was to be on the Santa Cruise, especially since there was a possibility that the ghost of Left Hook Louie was present. He waited for a laugh that did not come.

"Yes indeed," he continued with a cough. "Let's get started." He cleared his throat. "Born into the poverty of Hell's Kitchen," he began, showing a slide of a two-year-old sitting on the steps of a tenement with his mother.

"Rags to riches," Luke whispered to Nora. "Here we go."

Nora made a face at him.

The first ten minutes of the lecture included a

series of slides showing Left Hook Louie earning money at whatever job he could get, starting at age eight. In one photo, he and his sister, Maria, had set up a shoe-shine business on the corner of Tenth Avenue and Forty-third Street in New York City. Maria was proudly holding up a sign that read FIVE CENTS A SHOE. WILL LOOK LIKE NEW.

Luke whispered, "A budding entrepreneur. Most people wear two shoes."

More slides followed. "Here's twelve-year-old Louie delivering a massive piece of ice. He had to drag it up five flights, but never a whimper," Brevers explained. "The brave little fellow didn't know that he was developing the muscles that would make him a champion boxer. While others, including his boyhood chum, Charley-Boy Pinto, turned to a life of crime . . ."

As one, Regan and Jack leaned forward in their seats. "Pinto?"

"Louie was very disappointed when his beloved sister, Maria, at age eighteen, married Pinto. Neither he nor his parents ever spoke to her again. Charley-Boy spent the last fifteen years of his life in a federal prison. But before that, he had taught his son all about his 'business.' That son, Anthony, became the well-known mobster Bull's-Eye Tony Pinto, a dangerous man you may have been hearing about in the news recently. Although he probably never met his uncle, the champion boxer-turned-bestselling author, he bears a remarkable resemblance to him, as you'll see."

Their photographs appeared side by side on the screen.

Regan heard two audible gasps behind her. She turned as Maggie and Ivy got up and made their way to the door.

The four Reillys followed them.

Ivy was trembling and Maggie's face was pale.

"There's a small lounge over here," Nora said. "Let's slip in there."

"I don't want to start trouble," Ivy said. "This would be terrible for the Commodore. I knew whoever I saw looked like Left Hook Louie. But when I see their pictures side by side I can see the difference. Tony Pinto is *definitely* the man I saw in the chapel! He's a mobster? What is he in trouble for now?"

"He ran away from his house in Miami to avoid going on trial," Regan explained.

Ivy went weak at the knees and grabbed Maggie's hand. "You saw him, too?"

"I believe I did," Maggie said quietly. She looked at Regan and Jack. "What are you going to do?"

"If word gets out, we may have a panic. We aren't *positive* Pinto is on board, and if he is, we don't know if he's armed. For the sake of the safety of everyone on the ship, what we know must stay right here," Jack said firmly.

"Why on earth would he be on this ship?" Ivy asked.

"Because if he makes it to Fishbowl Island, he can't be sent back to the States for prosecution," Regan told her.

"Then we'd better turn around and go back to Miami," Ivy squealed.

"They can announce the ship needs repairs," Nora suggested.

"Then people will get nervous that it'll sink!" Ivy protested.

"Not if you say it's a simple but necessary adjustment to the engine," Nora explained. "Half the major ships have had at least minor problems on their maiden voyages. People will understand."

"The only problem," Luke said, " is that if Tony Pinto *is* on board and counting on getting to Fishbowl Island, when he realizes we're turning around, what might he do?"

There was no answer to that question.

"There's Dudley," Regan said suddenly and hurried out to stop him. "We need to talk to you right away. We're right here in the piano lounge. Where's the Commodore?"

"The Commodore is at the entrance to the dining salon inviting people to the sunset service."

"Get him."

Dudley knew better than to ask why. "Right away, Regan," he assured her as he dashed off. A moment later, Dudley was entering the lounge followed by the Commodore and Alvirah and Willy.

Regan wasn't surprised to see Alvirah. Like a bloodhound, she could track down a trouble spot.

The Commodore's face brightened at the sight of Ivy, a look that lasted only seconds when she blurted out, "I'm sorry, Randolph, but the man I saw the other night is a criminal, and he's on this ship!"

"What?" the Commodore asked as the color drained from his face.

Regan closed the door to the lounge and apprised everyone of the situation.

"We'll never live this down!" the Commodore said. "But we must consider the safety of the passengers first. What do you suggest we do?"

"We really must go back to Miami, have the passengers disembark, and then the police will make a thorough search of the ship without the danger of some innocent person being hurt," Jack answered.

"What do we tell the passengers?" the Commodore asked him.

"That there's minor engine trouble, we are returning to Miami for a replacement part for the engine, and then we'll cruise the local waters off Miami until Thursday."

"We can always promise the passengers another free cruise," Dudley volunteered hysterically.

"Bite your tongue," the Commodore snapped. "You and your free cruise idea got me into all this trouble. From now on, keep your suggestions to yourself!"

Dudley wilted. "I just thought . . ." he began. "I was just trying to be helpful. . . ." He longed for the moment when he had thought falling off the rock-climbing wall was going to be the worst thing that happened to him on this ship. He wondered if other cruise lines would be hiring after the New Year.

"Dudley, get Captain Smith," the Commodore ordered. "I know he's already in the dining room."

Once again Dudley dashed off. Less than a minute later, he returned with Captain Smith, whose expression did not change when he heard the saga of the probable stowaway.

"I remember on one of my ship's maiden voyage we lost all power during a particularly vicious storm and were battered unmercifully by the waves for two days—"

"Yes, yes," the Commodore interrupted impatiently.

Dudley knew that only the Captain could match the Commodore in relating every last detail of an event that had happened years ago.

"So it is feasible that we could have an engine failure that could be temporarily corrected," the Captain continued. "I will go directly to the bridge now, begin to slow the ship, then toward the end of the lunch hour bring her to a complete stop. Then I will come up to the dining salon to ostensibly report the problem to you, Commodore."

The Commodore was thoughtful. "At which time I will explain what is happening to the passengers. I will also make the announcement that in view of the circumstances my dear mother's ceremony will begin at two thirty."

"I thought you wanted to have it at sunset?" Dudley interrupted.

"Not anymore! If we are turning back this is the nearest spot to where I had planned to leave Mother."

With a brief nod but without speaking, Captain Smith left them.

Alvirah was debating. Should they warn the Commodore not to say anything to Eric about Tony Pinto? But what would the reason be for it? Should she explain that Eric was looking for a deck of cards and might possibly be connected to Tony Pinto? That there were traces of mysterious potato chips on the carpet of his room that he never would have eaten? We can't tell him that, she decided. If Eric was guilty, his uncle would find out soon enough.

The Commodore squared his shoulders. "Our guests are beginning to have lunch. I must join them. Ivy, there's a place for you at my table." Taking her arm, he steered her to the door.

The others watched them leave.

"That's a classy guy," Luke commented.

"This could be the ruination of his cruise ship," Dudley said sadly. "His back is against the financial wall."

Nora sighed. "Well, we'd better go inside." She turned to Maggie. "Why don't you sit with us?" With a wry smile she added, "You're our co-conspirator."

"Thank you, but Ted is planning to sit at my table for lunch."

"Jack and I will be right back," Regan said as they started walking toward the door.

"I have to call the office and let them know what's going on." Jack's voice was crisp.

"Bring the cards back," Alvirah directed them. "Eric is bugging us for them."

"We will," Regan assured her.

Regan and Jack turned toward the elevators. The others walked into the dining salon. Fifteen minutes later, Regan and Jack were hurrying toward the table.

"What?" Alvirah asked before they even sat down.

Regan's voice was low. "We just learned that there is a close connection between Bull's-Eye Tony Pinto and Barron Highbridge, the classy crook from Greenwich who ran a huge investment scam and was about to be sentenced. Highbridge disappeared last week, and his ex-girlfriend is sure he called her from Miami. His gofer is a cousin of Bingo Mullens, the guy the police are sure arranged Bull's-Eye's escape."

"What does Highbridge look like?" Alvirah asked.

"Tall and thin," Regan answered.

"Like the one-belled Santa who left me high and dry on the deck!" Alvirah cried.

Jack took the cards out of his pocket and slid them across the table. "You can give the cards back to Eric," he said. "My office is pretty sure these are numbers of Swiss bank accounts. They're working on it and will know soon."

Alvirah said flatly, "The big question is, 'What were those cards doing in *Eric's* room?'"

# 49

Eric could not believe what was going on. The ship was now at a complete stop and would soon be turning back to port. I'm a dead man, he thought despairingly. If I can't get those two off the ship, and they get caught when we dock in Miami, Bull's-Eye will definitely have me killed. Even if I'm in jail, he'll find a way. . . . Eric could not believe how stupid he had been. If I had just helped Uncle Randolph make this operation work, I could have had a good life, he thought. I'm his only heir. There would have been lots of money, lots of single girls on the cruises—I could have had everything.

No matter what, I've *got* to get those two off the ship!

He hurried up to the suite and opened the door of his room. While he was still debating what to tell the two escapees in his closet, Eric heard the door from the corridor open and realized that the Commodore had followed him.

Eric turned to him. "Uncle Randolph, I can't tell you how sorry I am that we have to go back to Miami. I know how awful it is for you, with the bad publicity we're already getting."

The Commodore sat heavily on the couch and buried his face in his hands. "My boy," he said, "it's worse. *Much* worse."

What could be worse? Eric wondered as he felt his entire body burst into a sweat. "What is it?" he managed to croak.

"We are virtually certain we have a mobster on board as a stowaway—the so-called Bull's-Eye Tony Pinto."

"Wha . . . wha . . . what?" Eric stammered.

"There is no engine problem. We're only saying that to avoid a panic among the passengers. As you must know, Jack Reilly is the head of the Major Case Squad in New York City. We are following his advice. We will return to Miami, and the police will search from one end of this ship to the other. Wait till I find out where he's been hiding and who's been hiding him." The Commodore's voice rose. "Give me two minutes with that crook in a locked room! I'll show *him* what a Bull's-Eye is!"

Eric cringed. Bull's-Eye and Highbridge are listening to this, he thought. At least I don't have to break the news to them. He remembered an expression of his grandmother's, "We get comfort wherever we can find it." Eric looked at the locked glass case where his grandmother's ashes were reposing in the silver box. You never liked me, he thought. That's why I turned out the way I did.

The Commodore stood. "The ceremony will begin very soon," he said. "We are going to make it short and sweet, then the Captain will start the engines and we'll head home. I'm going to spend these last precious moments with Grandma in the chapel."

As soon as his uncle was gone, Eric went into his room and shut the door. His palms so sweaty he could barely open the door of the closet, he braced himself and turned the handle.

"I'd kill you now, but we still need you," Bull's-Eye said with no emotion in his voice.

"We have to get off the ship while it's stopped," Highbridge told Eric. "Give me your satellite phone. Get the reading of the latitude and longitude. We'll call our people and tell them to find us in your dinghy. They can figure out how far we'd drift."

Bull's-Eye reached in the pocket of his Santa suit and pulled out Crater's gun. "All the cash we gave you is coming with us, too." Eric looked up at the shelf and realized that his locked suitcase had been pried open.

"We were looking for our clothes," Bull's-Eye explained. "Too bad you weren't smart enough to put our deposit for this trip in the bank. Forget about it. It would have been easier to swim than to put up with your plans. And I'm not leaving without my cards," he said flatly.

Eric ran out to his uncle's desk, checked the latitude and longitude of the ship, then hurried back and reported the readings to Highbridge. "While you make the call, I'll get the cards," he promised desperately. He closed the doors of the closet and of his bedroom, hurried through the suite, and went out into the corridor. He was about to go to the Meehans' door and knock when he glanced down toward the elevator bank. They were just stepping off the elevator. He waited for them and to his vast relief he didn't even have to ask about the cards.

"Oh, Eric," Alvirah said, "we have your friend's cards."

Willy piped up. "Tell your buddy if he's getting together a game, I'd love to join him."

Eric's palms were sweaty as he closed them around Bull's-Eye's cards. "Sure, sure, I'll tell him. Thanks." His eyes briefly registered the chocolate syrup stains covering the front of Willy's shirt.

Willy laughed. "Don't think I'm a slob. The waiter was being generous, but in my case he missed my bowl of ice cream when he was ladeling out the hot fudge sauce. I'm on my way to change."

"Sorry about that," Eric said, his grip on the cards so tight that they were cutting into his palm.

"See you at your grandmother's ceremony," Alvirah said as they continued down the corridor.

Eric waited until the Meehans were safely inside their stateroom. I need thirty seconds to get Bull's-Eye and Highbridge to the crew companionway, he reasoned. It led directly down to the stern, where he had hidden the dinghy. It was risky using the stairs now, but even if they passed a crew member he would know better than to question Eric or anyone with him. Eric worried that Winston might be a problem—he used those stairs all the time to get down to his cabin and had a way of appearing out of nowhere.

Eric knew that he had to get Bull's-Eye and Highbridge down to the open area on the lowest deck at the stern where nets, hooks, and assorted waterproof paraphernalia for the ship were stored. There was no concealed locker or closet, which was why he had not even considered hiding the two men there. But there *was* an overhang, which meant no one from the upper decks could see what was happening there from above. The risk was that someone would spot them when they threw the inflatable dinghy over the stern in broad daylight. Once the two men were in the dinghy, Eric had a canvas cover they could pull over themselves so that anyone who saw the dinghy would assume it was empty. But hopefully everyone would be at his grandmother's ceremony.

Eric went back into the suite, strode to his room, and opened the door of his closet. He handed Bull's-Eye the cards. "Let's go," he snapped, noticing that Bull's-Eye had the briefcase he must have stolen and Highbridge was holding Eric's duffel bag to which they'd obviously transferred the cash they'd given Eric and their clothing.

"Coming," Bull's-Eye snapped back.

By the grace of God, they made it to the crew companionway without running into anyone. What they didn't know was that Alvirah's ear was at the slightly opened door of her room. When she heard the Commodore's door shut, she poked out her head just in time to see Eric and the two Santas disappear behind the unmarked door at the other end of the passageway. It was the door she had seen Winston use, and she was sure it was intended just for the crew.

Merciful heavens! she thought. That has to be Bull's-Eye and the Santa I was chasing. Eric is hand-in-glove with them! I can't waste a second. Willy's in the shower, but if I take the time to tell him what's up it'll be too late and I'll lose them. She bolted down the corridor as fast as her arthritic knees would permit, silently opened the door they'd gone through, and could hear their footsteps in the distance, echoing several decks below. She grabbed the railing as she hurried after them.

When she reached the bottom deck, there was a metal door to her left. She opened it a crack. A rubber dinghy was being inflated, and two men were strapping life jackets over their Santa suits.

I've got to get help, she thought. She turned and started up the stairs, but before she had gone six steps the door flew open behind her. She tried to run faster, but it was impossible to escape. She felt a strong hand clamp over her mouth, a muscled arm pull her back, and heard Eric say, "You're not *that* good an amateur sleuth, Mrs. Meehan."

# 50

Crater had panicked when Fredericka and Gwendolyn had informed him once again that the time of the ceremony had been changed. He had placed an urgent call to his people. "There can be no delays!"

"Don't worry. We're almost there," he was told.

Crater had then informed Dr. Gephardt that he had sent for his helicopter. "With the breakdown of the ship, I don't feel comfortable, and I can tell from previous experiences that a major asthma attack is building up. My breathing is getting shorter. I want to go home, where good medical care is close at hand."

What a load of bull, Dr. Gephardt had thought, sitting in his office and twirling a pencil as he listened.

"But I *am* looking forward to the ceremony for the Commodore's mother. Those lovely children who have been so kind to me will be singing, I understand."

"So I heard," Dr. Gephardt said, thinking how glad he'd be when Crater was gone. Whoever tried to smother him could have another go at it. Jack Reilly might be interested in this, Gephardt thought as he hung up. He dialed the Reilly's stateroom, but there was no answer.

On the top deck, at the bow of the ship, people were already gathering for the ceremony. Crew members had placed rows of folding chairs on either side of a makeshift aisle through which the Commodore, Eric, and the Santa Claus guard of honor would march. A small table from the Commodore's suite had been placed in front of the crowd, a bouquet of flowers and a hand microphone on it. Stereo speakers had been set up to play "Amazing Grace."

The sun was bright, the sea calm, the only movement of the *Royal Mermaid* being caused by the waves gently lapping against it.

In the distance, the sound of a helicopter approaching caught everyone's attention. A buzz went through the ship, and in an instant the deck was full. Dudley came running out and rushed to pick up the microphone. "There is no need for alarm!" he began. "Our friend Mr. Crater," he nodded to Crater sitting in a wheelchair at the end of the front row near the rail, "needs to get home to consult with his family physician."

"Louder!" someone yelled. "We can't hear you!"

Dudley put his fingers to his lips and pointed at the helicopter. They all watched as it slowly settled on the helipad—engines roaring and blades whipping not far from where the ceremony was to take place.

Fredericka and Gwendolyn, standing on either side of the wheelchair, covered Crater's ears with their palms. The remaining seats in the left front row were reserved for the Commodore, Eric, Dudley, and Winston. The front row on the other side of the aisle was reserved for the Santas.

The roaring of the helicopter's engine abruptly stopped and the rotation of the blades slowed until they no longer moved. Dudley quickly repeated what he'd explained before and then said, "We'll be starting our lovely tribute to Mrs. Penelope Weed in just a few moments. Please take your seats."

The four Reillys, Ivy, and Maggie were seated in the second row. They had saved two seats for Willy and Alvirah, but Willy came out on the deck by himself. His face fell when he saw that Alvirah wasn't with them.

"Where's Alvirah?" he asked worriedly.

"We haven't seen her," Nora told him.

"She was gone from the room when I got out of the shower. I was surprised, but I figured she'd come out here."

"Oh, I'm sure she'll be right along," Nora said soothingly.

All eyes focused on the helicopter as three men in medical scrubs climbed out. Dudley ran over to greet them.

"Something doesn't feel right," Regan whispered to Jack.

Jack's eyes narrowed as he watched the three medics follow Dudley to Crater's wheelchair. They leaned over and had a brief chat with him. Jack noticed one of the medics look over and make eye contact with Winston. They know each other, he thought. What's that about?

The opening notes of "Amazing Grace" blared from the speakers, startling everyone.

The procession arrived from the chapel. The two Santa Clauses who didn't have outfits came down the aisle first, each carrying a tall, lighted candle. The eight costumed Santas followed, then Eric, and finally the Commodore carrying the silver box with his mother's ashes.

Regan stared at Eric as the congregation sang. "That saved a wretch like me . . ."

Willy had taken his seat but was noticeably upset.

269

The Commodore placed the silver box on the table between the two lighted candles as the members of the procession took their places in the front row.

A thin, middle-aged man from the Oklahoma Readers and Writers group, who was a deacon in his church back home, came forward. He picked up the microphone. "Merciful God, life has not ended, but changed," he began.

Willy turned and looked to the back of the rows of chairs, desperate for any sight of Alvirah. He was sure that she would never deliberately miss this ceremony. She just wouldn't. He knew it in his bones.

Something must have happened to her.

# 51

When Eric dragged Alvirah back down the companionway, and out onto the deck, Bull's-Eye ripped off his beard and tied it as a makeshift gag around her mouth. Highbridge pulled her hands behind her back and used his Santa cap to secure them. Eric then pushed her down on the floor, against a wall covered with nets and fishing equipment. "I've got to get out of here. I can't be late for the ceremony. The last thing we need is for them to start looking for me. Take good care of her," he snarled. "She's too nosy for her own good. And on top of that, she's the reason we had to move out of my room."

He's such a coward, Alvirah thought contemptuously as she watched him go. He doesn't want to kill me. He's leaving it to them.

Bull's-Eye trained his gun on her. "If you're so nosy, tell me what that two-bit punk Crater is doing on the ship. He's here for a reason, and it has nothing to do with him being a do-gooder," Bull's-Eye spat. "He ratted on my father. What's he planning now?"

"I wish I knew," Alvirah answered.

"I'll give you a minute to think about it before I whack you."

The sound of an approaching helicopter startled all three of them.

"That could be the cops." Highbridge's voice was panicked. He and Bull's-Eye shifted into high gear. As they threw the dinghy off the back of the ship Alvirah frantically began to twist her hands. She felt some kind of hook or sharp metal poking into her right side. Turning her body slightly, she moved just enough so that her bound hands were covering it. If I can just get a tear in the cap, she thought anxiously, it's thin, cheap material. The one bell at the end of the cap tinkled faintly, but Bull's-Eye and Highbridge were too distracted to hear it.

Bull's-Eye dropped a briefcase into a duffel bag and re-knotted the bag tightly.

Trying to remain calm, Alvirah moved the cap back and forth over the metal until she made a hole in it. Thinking back to her cleaning days when she used to tear up old towels into rags, she was finally able to shred the cap and free her hands.

Alvirah eyed the low railing on the side of the ship. I can do it, she thought. I have to do it. I'm not ready to leave Willy on his own yet. He needs me. Getting up off the floor is the big problem. It takes me so long I may not get the chance to jump. But I've got to give it a try.

Highbridge climbed up and sat on the rail at the stern, facing the water.

Alvirah watched as Bull's-Eye hoisted the duffel bag onto the railing and Highbridge wrapped his right hand around the top of it. Bull's-Eye then handed him an oar. "Don't drop anything. Especially the bag. I'll be right behind you."

"I'm not careless when it comes to protecting my money," Highbridge answered, then pushed himself off the edge. Bull's-Eye, a gun in his right hand, watched Highbridge's descent.

Alvirah heard a splash as Highbridge hit the water. Bull's-Eye's attention was riveted on the duffel bag as he made sure it arrived safely onto the dinghy.

It's now or never, Alvirah realized. Hardly feeling the twisting pangs in her knees, she sprang up, raced to the side of the ship, climbed on the rail, and, as a startled Bull's-Eye turned his head toward her, she held her nose and jumped. Immediately before she hit the water, she heard a bullet whistle past her ear. That was close, she thought, but no bull's-eye.

Her body completely submerged, she began to swim underwater toward the bow of the ship.

# 52

One of the few people who did not attend the ceremony was Bosley P. Brevers, who was upset because his lecture had seemed to have been a failure. The very people he was hoping to impress, the famous suspense writer and her husband, their daughter, the private investigator, and her husband, the big shot with the NYPD, had walked out in a block. He knew they were trying to be discreet, but the sight of the backs of their heads was very disconcerting. Those two women from his group, Maggie and Ivy, clearly couldn't stand him getting any attention. They had walked out first.

It was so mean of them.

He'd retreated to his cabin, where he'd ordered a sandwich from room service, then gone over his notes to see how he might make part two of his lecture more interesting. He had just put his pen down when he heard a helicopter approaching the ship. Stepping out onto his balcony to catch a glimpse, he quickly became disinterested and went back inside his room to turn on the television. He wanted to see if there was any news on the search for Left Hook Louie's nephew, Tony Pinto. If the police caught him, that would bring some fresh excitement to the lecture scheduled for tomorrow morning. As Brevers flipped the channels, he could hear the faint sounds of "Amazing Grace." Obviously the Commodore's ceremony had begun.

A clip of a pretty young newscaster appeared on the screen. "Update!" she said excitedly. "I've been reporting to you about the Santa Cruise on the *Royal Mermaid,* which used to belong to the late Angus 'Mac' MacDuffie. It's been verified that years ago MacDuffie's father bought a priceless antique knowing it had been stolen from a Boston museum. A hammered silver jewelry box, it had once belonged to Cleopatra and is worth untold millions. That's right folks. Cleopatra! This morning, I visited the people who had purchased furniture and papers from the estate sale after Angus MacDuffie died. In a kneehole desk, they discovered a journal, which revealed that MacDuffie knew about the antique. Today, we painstakingly went through hundreds of dusty magazine pages and letters, and we found a note MacDuffie had written to his mother saying that he had hidden the stolen silver box in a secret drawer he had built in the suite of his yacht so that evidence of his father's disgrace would die with him. Maybe Commodore Weed will start a treasure hunt . . ."

A replica of the box flashed on-screen.

Brevers's eyes bulged. He had been one of the first to arrive on the ship yesterday and had gone to the Commodore's suite to drop off a signed book. The Commodore had invited him into the living room and they had chatted briefly. Brevers had noticed an exquisite, small silver chest in a glass case against the wall and had commented on it. The Commodore had told him it contained his mother's ashes.

Could it be? Brevers wondered, his mind racing. He had heard this morning that the Commodore would be throwing his mother's ashes overboard in a box. Could it be the priceless object that he had just seen? The Commodore's silver box certainly looked like the one they were showing on television.

Not caring that he'd taken off his shoes, Brevers ran out the door and down the deserted corridor in what he believed was a race to save Cleopatra's jewelry box from disappearing to the bottom of the sea.

# 53

Good-byes are always so difficult, but the time has come to say a loving farewell to the best mother a boy every had. I'm so glad that you all could be with me to share this tender, albeit painful, moment." The Commodore nodded to Gwendolyn and Fredericka who stepped forward and began to sing.

"My Mommy lies over the ocean . . ."

The Commodore turned and began to walk toward the railing, the silver chest in hand.

Alvirah held her breath as long as she could until, her lungs bursting, she had to come up for air. This water doesn't feel tropical to me, she thought. The beard was choking her. With one hand she grabbed it, and even though it had been tightly knotted around her mouth, she managed to yank it down. Gasping and freezing, she looked over her shoulder. All they care about is getting away now, she thought thankfully. They haven't got time to worry about me.

Though the ship was stopped, the current was moving it slightly forward. The distance to the bow seemed farther and farther away.

Her slacks and sandals felt as though they weighed a ton. She tried to kick off her sandals, but the effort was pulling her down. Just swim, she thought. Stay afloat and swim.

A wave washed over her face, causing her to sputter and swallow water. "Willy," she tried to call. By now I'm sure he's worried. But he won't think to look over the railing for me.

Oh, Willy, if that dopey waiter hadn't dribbled hot fudge all over you, you wouldn't have been in the shower when I saw those guys.

Her arms were so heavy. The ship looks as though it's moving forward. They say your life flashes before you when you're drowning, but all I can think of is how that hot fudge stained Willy's new blue shirt.

I love you, Willy.

One arm in front of the other, ever more slowly, she forced herself to keep moving.

It happened in an instant. As the Commodore was slowly walking past Crater's wheelchair, Brevers came running down the deck.

"Don't throw that box overboard!" he shouted. "It's worth *millions!*"

Like a shot, Crater jumped out of his wheelchair.

I'm getting closer, Alvirah promised herself, I'm getting closer. Her arms felt like lead. It was getting harder and harder to pull air into her lungs. She was shivering from head to foot. She was almost at the bow, praying that there were people up there. She looked up and saw three men standing directly above her. "Help!" she tried to call, but her voice came out a croaking whisper.

And then, just as she thought they would spot her, the men hurried away from the railing.

The shock of hearing Brevers's frantic outcry was followed by the equally astonishing sight of Crater wrestling the silver box from the Commodore's arms.

The helicopter's engine was suddenly turned on and its blades began to whir.

Regan and Jack sprang to their feet.

"This is preposterous," the Commodore cried as Crater gained possession of his mother's ashes and, like a football player making a forward pass, tossed the chest to one of his medics who caught it and turned to run for the helicopter.

Fredericka, annoyed that her singing had been interrupted, stuck out her foot. The medic tripped, crashed on the deck, and the box flew from his grasp. By then Regan, Jack, Luke, Willy, and the ten Santa Clauses were galvanized into action. A sea of red suits knocked Crater down and surrounded the fallen medic. The other two raced for the safety of the helicopter.

"Nice try," Jack shouted as he and Ted tackled the two men.

As the melee ensued, the silver chest was, for the moment, unguarded on the deck. Winston ran over, scooped it up, and started for the helicopter. Gwendolyn, always in competition with her sister, and the fastest runner in her gym class, was right behind him. She dove for his legs and he, too, went sprawling. Grabbing the silver box as Winston released his grip on it, she ran to the rail and shouted, "This isn't nice! The Commodore wanted his Mommy to go into the sea right here!!!" Curling her tongue, she lifted the chest over her head and determinedly threw it as far as she could over the side of the ship.

Regan raced over to the rail. "Oh, my God!" she screamed as she looked out and saw that the airborne box was headed not only for the ocean, but also for Alvirah's head. "Watch out, Alvirah!"

she shrieked, then looked around wildly. She spotted a round, white life preserver hanging on a hook nearby, grabbed it, climbed over the rail, and jumped.

"Regan!" Nora screamed.

"Grab that box!" Brevers cried. "It's priceless!"

An exhausted Alvirah, who always knew the value of a dollar, reached out and with a mighty stretch of her arms caught the box as it hit the water. A moment later, Regan was pushing the life preserver in front of her. "Hang on to this, Alvirah," she ordered.

Alvirah passed the silver chest to Regan, then wrapped her arms around the life preserver that read SANTA CRUISE in bold lettering.

"This is what I get for giving to charity," Alvirah tried to joke, attempting to catch her breath. "I told you this trip would be exciting." Her arms were so numb and cold she felt herself starting to slip. "I don't know whether I can hold on—"

A strong arm encircled her waist. "I've got you, Alvirah," Jack said.

"You two never let me down," Alvirah breathed. "Is Willy all right?"

"He'll be a lot better when we get you back on the ship," Jack answered.

Alvirah felt faint. "One more thing," she whispered urgently. "Bull's-Eye and Highbridge are in a dinghy at the back of the ship, trying to get away. Eric is their accomplice."

Relieved that she was in the safe hands of her good friends, and that justice would be served, Alvirah allowed herself to pass out.

# 54

*Friday, December 30th*

Three days later, the Santa Cruise, minus all the known criminals who had been on board, was sailing into the Port of Miami.

Alvirah and Willy, Regan and Jack, Luke and Nora, Ivy, Maggie, Ted Cannon, Bosley Brevers, and Gwendolyn and Fredericka, accompanied by their doting parents, were having a farewell visit with the Commodore in his suite. Dudley and Dr. Gephardt were also in attendance.

The Commodore looked at the glass cabinet where once again his mother's ashes were reposing. They were in the original urn, which he had kept inside the silver chest. The policemen who had swarmed onto the ship an hour after the melee had been in the waters nearby investigating a potential drug smuggling operation. They had been given a false lead and were about to head back to Miami when they received the call about the Santa Cruise. Aside from all the assorted law-

284

breakers, they had also taken charge of Cleopatra's jewelry box. On loan to the Boston museum when it was stolen, the priceless antique would soon be on its way back to Egypt.

"I'll keep Mother with me until the next cruise," the Commodore said for the umpteenth time in the past seventy-two hours. "It's clear she wasn't intended to go yet. But how she would have loved to have known she was resting in Cleopatra's jewelry box!" He shook his head. "My mother never did cotton to Eric. And quite frankly, much as I tried, neither did I. It really hurt me when I found out how thoroughly he betrayed me. A good stint in prison will make him realize the error of his ways. But I *really* cannot believe that my ex-wife Reeney, to whom I was *most* generous, was the one who planned the heist of the silver box, even going so far as to plant Winston in my midst. It is absolutely galling! I knew she liked antiques, but to think that she was the brains behind a gang that had been buying and selling stolen antiquities for years is unbelievable! She never blinked an eye when I showed her the silver box and explained that I just happened upon it when I was rummaging through that lower cabinet in my suite and released some sort of spring that opened a panel. All she said was that it was a cute little box. 'Cute!' she said. She called it cute!"

Fredericka jumped up and put her arm around the Commodore, effectively halting his narrative, which by now was familiar fare to the others. "Don't be sad, Uncle Randolph. We're your family now."

"Forever!" Gwendolyn cried.

"I know you are," the Commodore said gently, his voice breaking.

Some more than others, Alvirah thought as she saw the tender look he exchanged with Ivy. She also noticed that Maggie and Ted's fingers were entwined as they sat side by side on the couch. This ship has turned into the Love Boat, she thought happily.

Dudley jumped in before the Commodore could get started again. He held up his glass. "I propose a toast. To all of you who have made this cruise so special, so memorable," he began.

Willy looked at Alvirah. "Memorable?" he muttered. "Is he kidding?"

"Afraid not," Alvirah answered, smiling at her husband. He hadn't left her side since she was plucked out of the water three days ago.

"I heard that," Dudley laughed. "It has been memorable. Memorable, yet wonderful. Wonderful to have you all as our new friends. I'm sure the Commodore will agree that you are always welcome as our guests on the *Royal Mermaid.*"

There he goes again, the Commodore thought with amusement. Giving away what isn't his.

"But make your plans fast," Dudley continued. "With all the excitement, reservations are pouring in. Our first four cruises are already totally booked."

Regan caught the expression on her father's face. She smiled. She knew what he was thinking: "Lucky for us." She turned to Jack. He winked at her. She could tell he was thinking the exact same thing. Well, we are lucky, Regan mused. Lucky about a lot of things.

Twenty minutes later they were standing on the sun-splashed deck as the pilot boat guided them into the dock. A beaming Bianca Garcia greeted the Santa Cruise, an adventure that had launched her onto the national news scene. Her station had hired a small band. As the ship glided to a halt, the band began to play "Auld Lang Syne."

The passengers, all of whom had enjoyed an unforgettable trip, joined in song.

"We'll drink a cup of kindness now. . . ."

The voyage of the Santa Cruise had come to an end—and a new year was about to begin.

# I Heard
# That Song
# Before

*by*

## MARY HIGGINS CLARK

# Prologue

My father was the landscaper for the Carrington estate. With fifty acres, it was one of the last remaining private properties of that size in Englewood, New Jersey, an upscale town three miles west of Manhattan via the George Washington Bridge.

One Saturday afternoon in August twenty-two years ago, when I was six years old, my father decided, even though it was his day off, that he had to go there to check on the newly installed outside lighting. The Carringtons were having a formal dinner party that evening for two hundred people. Already in trouble with his employers because of his drinking problem, Daddy knew that if the lights placed throughout the formal gardens did not function properly, it might mean the end of his job.

Because we lived alone, he had no choice except to take me with him. He settled me on a bench in the garden nearest the terrace with strict instructions to stay right there until he came back. Then he added, "I may be a little while, so if you have to use the bathroom, go through the screen door around the corner. You'll see the staff powder room just inside it."

That sort of permission was exactly what I needed. I had heard my father describe the inside of the great stone mansion to my grandmother, and my imagination had gone wild visualizing it. It had been built in Wales in the seventeenth century and even had a hidden chapel where a priest could both live and celebrate Mass in secrecy during the era of Oliver Cromwell's bloody attempt to erase all traces of Catholicism from England. In 1848 the first Peter Carrington had the mansion taken down and reassembled stone by stone in Englewood.

I knew from my father's description that the chapel had a heavy wooden door and was located at the very end of the second floor.

I had to see it.

I waited five minutes after he disappeared into the gardens and then raced through the door he had pointed out. The back staircase was to my immediate right, and I silently made my way upstairs. If I did encounter anyone, I planned to say that I was looking for a bathroom, which I persuaded myself was partially true.

On the second floor, with rising anxiety I tiptoed down one carpeted hallway after another as I encountered a maze of unexpected turns. But then I saw it: the heavy wooden door my father had described, so out of place in the rest of the thoroughly modernized house.

Emboldened by my luck in having encountered no one in my adventure, I ran the last few steps and rushed to open the door. It squeaked as I tugged at it, but it opened just enough for me to squeeze through.

Being in the chapel was like going back in time. It was much smaller than I'd expected. I had pictured it as similar to the Lady Chapel in St. Patrick's Cathedral, where my grandmother always stopped to light a candle for my mother, on the rare occasions when we shopped in New York. She never failed to tell me how beautiful my mother had looked the day she and my father were married there.

The walls and floor of this chapel were built of stone, and the air I was breathing felt damp and cold.

A nicked and peeling statue of the Virgin Mary was the room's only religious artifact, and a battery-lit votive candle in front of it provided the only dim and shadowy lighting. Two rows of wooden pews faced the small wooden table that must have served as an altar.

As I was taking it all in, I heard the door begin to squeak and I knew someone was pushing it open. I did the only thing I could do—I ran between the pews and dropped to the ground, then ostrichlike buried my face in my hands.

From the voices I could tell that a man and a woman had entered the chapel. Their whispers, harsh and angry, echoed against the stone. They were arguing about money, a subject I knew well. My grandmother was always sniping at my father, telling him that if he kept up the drinking there wouldn't be a roof over his head or mine.

The woman was demanding money, and the man was saying that he already had paid her enough. Then she said, "This will be the last time, I swear," and he said, "I heard that song before."

I know my memory of that moment is accurate. From

the time I could understand that, unlike my friends in kindergarten, I did not have a mother, I had begged my grandmother to tell me about her, every single thing she could remember. Among the memories my grandmother shared with me was one of my mother starring in the high school play and singing a song called "I Heard That Song Before." "Oh, Kathryn, she sang it so beautifully. She had a lovely voice. Everyone clapped so long and shouted, *'encore, encore.'* She had to sing it again." Then my grandmother would hum it for me.

Following the man's remark, I could not hear the rest of what was said except for her whispered, "Don't forget," as she left the chapel. The man had stayed; I could hear his agitated breathing. Then, very softly, he began to whistle the tune of the song my mother sang in the school play. Looking back, I think he may have been trying to calm himself. After a few bars, he broke off and left the chapel.

I waited for what seemed forever, then I left, too. I hurried down the stairs and back outside, and, of course, never told my father that I'd been in the house or what I had heard in the chapel. But the memory never faded, and I am sure of what I heard.

Who those people were, I don't know. Now, twenty-two years later, it is important to find out. The only thing that I have learned for certain, from all of the accounts of that evening, is that there were a number of overnight guests staying in the mansion, as well as five in household help, and the local caterer and his crew. But that knowledge may not be enough to save my husband's life, if indeed it deserves to be saved.

# LACED

*by*
## CAROL HIGGINS CLARK

*Monday, April 11th*

In a remote village in the west of Ireland, a light mist rose from the lake behind Hennessy Castle. The afternoon was becoming increasingly gray and brooding as clouds gathered and the skies turned threatening. Inside the castle the fireplaces were lit, providing a cheery warmth for the guests who were already anticipating a wonderful evening meal in the elegant eighteenth-century dining room.

The massive front doors of the castle opened slowly, and newlyweds Regan and Jack Reilly stepped out onto the driveway in their jogging clothes. They'd arrived on an overnight flight from New York, slept for several hours, and decided a quick jog might help alleviate the inevitable jet lag.

Jack looked at his thirty-one-year-old bride, touched her hair, and smiled. "We're in our native land, Mrs. Reilly. Our Irish roots lie before us."

Anyone who saw the handsome couple wouldn't have questioned those roots. Jack was six foot two, with sandy hair, hazel eyes, a firm jaw, and a winning smile. Regan had blue eyes, fair skin, and dark hair—she was one of the black Irish.

"Well, it certainly is green around here," Regan observed as she glanced around at the lush gardens, wooded trails, and rolling lawn. "Everything is so still and quiet."

"After last week, still and quiet sounds good to me," Jack said. "Let's go."

Together they broke into a jog and crossed a pedestrian bridge that traversed a stream in front of the castle. They turned left and headed down an isolated country road that the concierge told them led right into the village. The only sound was their sneakers hitting the pavement. At a curve in the road they passed an old stone church that looked deserted.

Regan pointed toward the steepled building. "I'd love to take a look in there tomorrow."

Jack nodded. "We will." He glanced up at the sky. "I think that rain is coming in faster than we expected. This jog is going to be quick."

But when the road ended at the tiny village, a graveyard with darkened gravestones proved irresistible to Regan. A set of stone steps to their left led up to a courtyard where a broken stone wall surrounded the cemetery. "Jack, let's take a quick look."

"The funeral director's daughter," Jack said affectionately. "You never met a graveyard you didn't like."

Regan smiled. "Those tombstones must be centuries old."

They hurried up the steps, turned right, and

stopped in their tracks. The first tombstone they spotted said REILLY.

"This is a good omen," Jack muttered.

Regan leaned forward. "May Reilly. Born in 1760 and died in 1822. There don't seem to be any other Reillys here with her."

"Just as long as there aren't any named Regan or Jack."

Regan was deep in thought. "You know that joke my father always tells? The one about how an Irishman proposes?"

"You want to be buried with my mother?"

"That's the one. It looks like poor May didn't have anyone, not even a mother-in-law."

"Some people would consider that a good thing." Jack grabbed Regan's hand as large drops of rain started to come down. "Tomorrow we'll spend as much time as you want here figuring out what went wrong in these people's lives. Come on."

Regan smiled. "I can't help it. I'm an investigator."

"So am I."

They didn't encounter a single soul as they ran through the tiny village, which consisted of a pharmacy, two pubs, a souvenir shop, and a butcher. They wound around and jogged back to the castle where they showered and changed.

At 7:30 they went down to dinner and were seated at a table by a large window overlooking the garden. The rain had stopped, and the night was peaceful. Their waiter greeted them warmly.

"Welcome to Hennessy Castle. I trust you're enjoying yourselves so far."

"We certainly are," Regan answered. "But we stopped by the graveyard in town, and the first tombstone we saw had our name on it."

"Reilly?"

"Yes."

The waiter whistled softly. "You were looking at old May Reilly's grave. She was a talented lacemaker who supposedly haunts the castle, but we haven't heard from her for a while."

"She haunts this place?" Regan asked.

"Apparently May was always complaining that she wasn't appreciated. One of her lace tablecloths is in a display case upstairs in the memorabilia room. She made it for a special banquet of dignitaries who were visiting the Hennessy family, but May got sick and died before they paid her. Legend is that she keeps coming back for her money."

"Sounds like one of my cousins," Jack said.

"I don't blame her," Regan protested. "She should have been paid."

At 4:00 A.M. Regan woke with a start. Jack was sleeping peacefully beside her. The rain had started up again and sounded as if it was coming down harder than before. Regan slipped out of bed and crossed the spacious room to close the window. As she pulled back the curtain, a flash of lightning streaked across the sky. Regan looked down and in the distance saw the figure of a woman dressed in a long black coat, standing on the back lawn in front of the lake. She was staring up at Regan and shaking her fists. One hand was clenching a piece of white material. Could that be lace? Regan wondered.

"Regan, are you all right?" Jack asked.

Regan quickly turned her head away from the window, then just as quickly turned it back. Another bolt of lightning lit up the sky.

The woman was gone.

Jack flicked on the light. "Regan, you look as if you just spotted a ghost."

Before she could answer, the smell of smoke filled their nostrils. A moment later the fire alarm went off.

"So much for peace and quiet," Jack said quickly. "Let's throw on some clothes and get out of here!"